THE
BRAMBLE
TREE

To Bob and JeAn
Tremethick,
Hope you like my
story! God Bless
you!

RANDY LEE PURDY

Randy Lee Purdy
Sept 10, 2020
THursday

ISBN 978-1-0980-3035-3 (paperback)
ISBN 978-1-0980-3036-0 (digital)

Christian Faith Publishing, Inc.
832 Park Avenue
Meadville, PA 16335
www.christianfaithpublishing.com

Printed in the United States of America

CHAPTER 1

Twenty-five-year-old Rory Bramble stumbled off of the main highway onto the dusty back roads of Tyler, Texas. The rumbling grayish clouds told him rain was on the way as the lean six-foot-one-inch youngster with shoulder-length brownish blonde hair flipped a quarter in the air and slapped it on the top of his other hand. "Tails." And with an optimistic grin, he turned and took the road going south.

Wearing blue knee-torn jeans and a dirty white T-shirt, his old tennis shoes were worn out and dirty. He carried an itchy wool blanket over his shoulder for sleeping on, and he stopped briefly to remove his dirty baseball cap and wipe the sweat from his forehead. He noticed the hot day was turning windy as the opposing wind that had begun to push against him had a strong smell of rain.

He looked behind him with some satisfaction that he had gotten this far; his travel was only by walking or by hitchhiking from truck drivers down the highway. Where he was going, he did not know, having just been released from a six-year obligation from the state prison in Texarkana. Taking a deep breath of air into his lungs, he knew he had to find cover for the night.

He put his old cap back on his head and began walking south down a freshly paved two-lane highway toward a town he had seen on a sign while in that last truck that said, "Tyler, Texas, 20 miles ahead." His stomach ached with hunger, and his mouth was dry; occasionally, he could find enough moisture in his throat to swallow and even lick his dry lips.

Feeling light-headed and a bit frightened that he might pass out, he decided to take a chance and go to the closest home or ranch property that he could find. The rain would come soon, and he was near to fainting. Several hours later, he saw a sign—that was desperately in need of a coat of paint—that read "LL Ranch = (Double)." Too tired to care what the "LL" meant, he hurriedly walked through the wide wooden gate and up the dirt road that had some overgrown grass on both sides of the way toward what looked to be the main house.

Before reaching the house, thunder cracked loudly, and the rain attacked him violently. He opened his mouth to let the wet rain sooth his thirst. He pulled the wool blanket over his head when an old blue truck with various dents in it pulled up alongside him. "Jump on the other side, young feller," a man spoke to him.

He ran around the truck without hesitation and opened the passenger door and jumped in soaking wet from the rain. He looked at the man. "Thank you, sir."

The man dressed as an old ranch hand smiled at him, holding out his hand. "It's nice to meet you, young man!"

Rory reached over and politely shook his hand, replying, "Nice to meet you, sir. I'm sorry I'm getting your truck seat wet."

"Think nothing of it."

They continued to drive up the dirt driveway toward the house. "What's your name, youngster?" the old man asked, keeping his eyes on the road ahead of him.

"Rory"—clearing his dry throat. "Rory Bramble"—he coughed and covered his mouth.

The old man briefly turned and looked at him curiously. "I'm John Tuttle, owner of this LL Ranch."—looking back at the road with both hands on the steering wheel. "What brings you to my ranch, son?"

Rory felt no reason to lie to this kind man; his lip quivered some as he answered, "I need a job, sir, and I'm so hungry. I'm willing to work for any food you might have extra, sir. Please…" He covered his face with his right hand almost feeling he would pass out.

Tuttle stopped the truck at the front door, put the gear shift in park, turned off the ignition, and looked at him without hesitation. "Come on in the house, son. I'll get you a hot meal, and you can rest up. Spread that wet blanket over that chair on the porch so it can dry."

Climbing out of the truck, both men walked up to the house and into the front door. Rory was astonished and almost afraid of the unknown weathered-looking home. He removed his cap and stuck it in his back pocket and tried to comb his hair with his hand.

"Follow me into the kitchen, Rory." John Tuttle walked with a slight limp.

Rory complied, walking behind the cowboy almost embarrassed it had been a long time since he had been in a home with a family. Watching John Tuttle's bowed legs walk in his cowboy boots reminded him of earlier years in his life with his father. When they entered the kitchen, he could smell a pleasant aroma of food cooking, and almost instantly, his spirits perked up. There was a cute girl about his age wearing an apron around her waist, stirring something in a kettle that boiled on the gas oven stovetop.

He quickly looked around the kitchen and saw flowered wallpaper that looked old and dingy and wood-slated floors; there was a beaded chandelier light that illuminated a bright white glow hanging above the dark varnished and shiny wooden table. Drinking from a cup sat an older gray-whiskered man with both of his elbows on the table, and he just stared at Rory with a look of surprise. Next to the man, he saw a baby that appeared to be no more than a year old sitting in a high chair.

He looked farther inside and saw a living room area with a large couch and several comfortable chairs and television sitting on a wooden table next to the living room window. Next to stairs that went to an upper level of the home, there was a large bookshelf built into the wall that housed three levels of various-sized books. Within seconds, he realized the only reason he was noticing these things is that he was used to seeing a jail cell with just a bed and a toilet and steel bars for the front window.

The girl stopped what she was doing and turned to look at him with an awkward look on her face, wondering why this strange young man was sizing up their home. "Father, who have you brought home with you," she asked, holding a large plastic spoon she had been stirring the pot.

"Mildred, Cooter, this is Rory Bramble. I found him walking up to our driveway not more than a few minutes ago." John Tuttle smiled as he took his cowboy hat off and hung it on a coatrack that stood upright next to the kitchen back door.

The girl and the older man looked at him with curiosity, noticing his worn and dirty clothing and dirty face. Cooter set his cup down and stood up, then walked over to the young man. "I'm Cooter, son," reaching out his hand to shake. "Most just call me ole Coot."

"I'm Rory, sir. I'm honored to make your acquaintance." He reached out and shook Cooter's hand.

"That's what John just said. Likewise, boy," Cooter answered. "Your hands are rough like you have done some work. Did I catch the name of Bramble?"

"Yes, sir," feeling faint, and his eyes were heavy from lack of sleep.

Cooter looked over at John Tuttle, and he shook his head as if to say, "No, don't say anything." Cooter smiled at the boy and then sat back down at the kitchen table.

Rory turned and looked at Millie, feeling embarrassed knowing he was dirty and probably smelled some, knowing he had not bathed in a week or better. She approached him and put out her hand, and they shook. Quickly, she turned back around and walked back to the stove, noticing how bad Rory smelled. "There's soap by the sink."

"Yes, ma'am," he answered with a sad look on his face, and he hung his head.

John Tuttle had poured himself a cup of coffee and sat down at the table. He took a drink and looked up at the young man who seemed withdrawn and uneasy. "Rory, go ahead, son. Wash your hands and face off and come sit here with us and eat."

"Yes, sir," he complied. They all watched his hands shake with weakness; he was near to blacking out.

John looked at Millie with a stern look. "Okay, honey, let's eat supper with our guest."

"Yes, Father." And she began serving up plates with significant portions of fried chicken, mashed potatoes, beans, and bread with butter.

Rory finished washing up and dried his face with a towel that hung next to the sink. Not wanting to put the dirty towel down at the pan, he kept it with him and walked over to the table and sat down across from Cooter and managed a smile to the baby.

John Tuttle sat at the head of the table, and Millie sat next to the baby after having served up the food. "Let's thank the Lord before we eat," he muttered as he folded his hands.

Rory looked around at everyone and then folded his hands and hung his head in compliance, listening to Mr. Tuttle say a prayer.

"Heavenly father, we are thanking you for this good food that you have blessed us with and for all of our wonderful blessings that you have bestowed upon our home and family. And we especially are thankful for this young man that you have sent to our home. May you keep him in your hands. Amen, amen." After he finished, he began eating.

"Jump right in, son. Don't be shy!" Cooter smiled at Rory.

"There's plenty more if this isn't enough," Millie added as she began spoon-feeding her baby out of a small jar of baby food while nibbling on her helping.

Rory began eating and drinking the coffee that the girl had poured for him into his cup. It all tasted so beautiful; he could slowly feel his strength coming back to him. He was so thankful and had loved the prayer Mr. Tuttle had spoken.

For ten minutes, they ate in silence except for the baby making baby noises that Rory seemed to take a liking with. He liked babies; it seemed to come naturally to him.

John Tuttle saw him smiling at the baby. "That's my grandson William. He's almost a year old now," he laughed.

Rory smiled, looking across the table at William and his mother. "I like children a lot. They are so pure and innocent. William seems very happy," he spoke.

"My Willie is good, and he'll grow up to be a good man. I'll see to that," Millie spoke up while she ate and tended to the baby.

"I'm sure of that, ma'am." Rory smiled, trying to make conversation. "His dad must be proud of him." No one spoke, and Rory felt kind of awkward. "I mean, if I had a son, I'd be the proudest father on earth." He smiled innocently, looking around the room.

John smiled at him. "I'm sure you would too."

Rory felt he had said something wrong. Cooter drank his coffee to wash down some of his food, and Mr. Tuttle ate with a happy expression on his face that appeared friendly. So Rory continued to eat his fill. And finally, Millie began talking to him. "So, where do you come from, Rory Bramble? I mean, I don't think I've seen you around at any of the clubs in Tyler." She casually glanced at him from time to time.

He felt a little uneasy, knowing they would eventually ask him. But still, he stammered a bit, trying to buy more time before they made him leave. "This is great cooking, Mildred. Thank you all so much!" And he hung his head.

Mr. Tuttle and Cooter caught right on but said nothing to him. Millie, on the other hand, pried him for more information. "Call me, Millie. Where do you come from?"

"Millie, maybe he feels uncomfortable right now, dear. Don't prod him," John spoke up.

"What?" she answered, looking challenged. "You bring a stranger into our house with my baby here, and I'm not supposed to know who he is or where he's from!"—appearing to get angry.

Cooter cleared his throat loudly and moved his eating utensils to make noise but said nothing, showing his irritation to her remarks.

Rory didn't want a fight, so he spoke up with watery eyes. "I just got released a week or so from the Texarkana prison." He looked around, and no one spoke. "I'm sorry that I did not tell you. I was just so hungry."

"Oh my gosh! Father, you brought a convict into our home with my Willie here."

"Millie, stop. Don't talk like that, especially at the kitchen table," Tuttle spoke up.

Rory looked around, seeing the atmosphere had suddenly changed, yet Mr. Tuttle and Cooter remained calm, but the girl had become upset. "I'll be leaving now. I am sorry." He stood up to leave.

"Sit down, son. You're a guest in my home, and I've not said that you have to leave." John gave a stern look to his daughter.

Rory sat back down, feeling very uncomfortable and could feel the tension he had brought on to the young lady and even more sorry that a baby had to be in the room with such anxiety.

"Do you feel like telling us why you were in jail?" John asked.

"Mr. Tuttle, you have brought me into your home and fed me, a total stranger. I figure you are entitled to hear what happened."

"Okay, son, we'll hear you out."

He looked at them. "My parents were killed in a car accident when I was fifteen years old. All I had ever known was that we had traveled all across the country following the rodeo circuits."

"The rodeo?" Millie asked.

"Yes," he answered. "My father was famous in his time as a bronco buster. His name was Campbell Bramble, and his friends called him Camp. My mother was Ellie."

Tuttle and Cooter looked at each other, silently. "Go on, son," John spoke up.

"One morning, I heard someone knocking at the door of our motel room. My parents had left me there to study my book, learning homeschool training they made me do." He took a breath and squinted his eyes, trying to hold back the tears that came anyway.

The highway patrol officer told me my parents had been killed in a car accident by a drunk driver. I didn't know what to say to them, and I sat down on the bed and cried for thirty minutes while several patrolmen gathered my things together. They told me because I was only fifteen years old, I had to go to a local orphanage." Using the towel, he kept from the kitchen, he wiped the tears from his eyes.

John Tuttle looked at him, feeling the boy's pain. "Rory, I must tell you, Cooter here and I knew your parents well."

"You did?" Millie spoke up. "Why didn't you tell me?"

"Mildred, please. I wasn't sure when he told me his name in the driveway. Hearing the boy speak about his parents, I do know now."

Cooter spoke up, "Son, Tuttle here and I competed with your dad in the circuit. Camp Bramble was one of the best there ever was, except for Reilly Rider."

Rory's eyes filled with tears. "You knew my parents?"

"Yes, so we did. It was about ten years ago we had heard about the car accident and felt terrible about it. I even knew they had a son. I saw you with them many times over the years. I'm sorry. I figured family would take you in after they died."

"I have no family to speak of. I spent three years in the orphanage getting beat up by the older kids until I learned to fight back. Made me bitter against people, I guess."

"How'd you end up in prison, son?" Cooter asked.

"Some of the kids I battled within the orphanage were released at the same time I was when I turned eighteen years old."

"Where did you go?" Millie asked.

"I traveled to Arkansas and Oklahoma. Tried different places to get involved with rodeos and such. That's all I knew how to do. People told me I was either too young or had no money to buy my tack or to travel with."

He took a drink of coffee. "So I acted desperately, I guess. I joined four or five others I had known in the orphanage and started transporting moonshine, illegal domestic birds, snakes—anything that wasn't supposed to come into this county."

Silence filled the room except for the baby making happy noises.

"Some Mexican's found our gang of drifters broke and hung out in clubs drinking. They offered a lot of us some money, cars, food, and sometimes paid the motel bills. We did what they asked and didn't question anything. We eventually got caught by the law, and I was sent to prison for six years."

"I've heard horror stories about prisons," Millie spoke up as she wiped her son's face with a napkin.

"The stories are all true. It was awful, and I don't ever want to go back."

"How did you survive the experience?" she asked.

"I had help, and I was taken under the wing of one of the older prisoners who had been a dear friend of my father by the name of

Reilly Rider. He was there for life and didn't want me to stay there, and he told me that my father, Campbell, had helped him in several ways when he was active in the rodeo circuit. He explained to me how Campbell was an advocate for the safe and humane treatment of rodeo animals. Campbell saw how some people abused horses and bulls to make them mean and terrible temperament animals. And he felt compassion for them, starting petitions to stop that treatment.

"He said Campbell and Ellie were also prominent muscular dystrophy advocates. His only sister was a beautiful lady that had developed the disease and was progressively getting worse. The local sheriff in the town they had lived in had eyes for her, wouldn't leave her alone, so he took care of that situation and eventually got life in prison."

"Goodness!" Cooter said.

"What?" Millie asked.

"Reilly Rider was the only one who ever came close to beating Camp Bramble. He was that good! The rider was one of the best there ever was in the rodeo circuit. Why, just the other day, I read his name in a magazine article."

Rory looked curious. "He never told me why he was in prison. Seemed ashamed of it. He did, however, have some pull with the warden. He got me special privileges working with the prison stock, and I was able to train the horses and rode Brahmas in local county prison rodeos. Reilly said it would keep my skills up, and someday it may help me when I got out of prison."

Tuttle spoke up. "Camp Bramble and his wife, Ellie, had many friends, yet none of them were there for you, son. I'm sorry."

"At least not when they died, John. But sounds like one of them helped the kid in jail," Cooter said. "Rider went to jail because some sheriff caused his sister unspeakable problems, and he tried to defend her. Chances are, the warden in prison knew the truth too." Cooter sipped his coffee.

CHAPTER 2

"I do know the warden liked him a lot." Rory added, "Reilly taught me much about animals and how to care for them. I owe him a lot and some others. There was also a burly big young man named Buck Thompson, who was also my good friend, and these two men protected me and got me out of prison with good time served."

Rory drank his coffee and wiped his mouth with the towel. "Ma'am, you're a wonderful cook, and I thank you kindly for everything. May I do the dishes for you?"

"Sure, that would be a nice change. Then I could take my son upstairs and put him to bed," she answered.

"You have a wonderful son too! I like him,"

She looked at Rory and smiled. "Thank you! Will you be staying the night with our family?"

John Tuttle spoke up, "I'd say he'll be staying on here for good if he so decides. We'd be honored to have Campbell and Ellie's son stay here with us." He gave a broad smile.

"What do you say, Rory Bramble? Would you stay on here with us?" Cooter asked with a happy grin on his face.

Rory burst out in tears and hugged John Tuttle and Cooter. "Sir, you're the dream I have dreamt about for years. To live on a working ranch and be part of a real family. I'll make you so very proud of me. I promise. I can rope, ride, shoe horses—everything you need."

Then he looked at Millie. "And I love to help with the dishes," smiling at her.

"Yippee!" Cooter yelled out, "John, this was the best supper I've had in a long time."

"Cooter, I believe you're right! Today has been a godsent moment for all of us," Tuttle cheerfully said, wiping the tears from his eyes.

"It appears our family just keeps on growing, Dad." Millie smiled and hugged her dad.

"Son, you can take the spare room upstairs if you like."

Rory looked around, then spoke, "Sir, do you have a bunkhouse for your workers?"

"Why, yes, but Cooter stays out there himself. Ever since we downsized the ranch because of financial problems, the few I had moved on to larger spreads around Tyler. Cooter likes to stay with the horses to keep them company at night."

"Well, I'd like to stay in the bunkhouse with Cooter. I don't think it's proper with a lady in the house with her baby, if you don't mind."

John Tuttle smiled and patted Rory on the back. "As you wish, son. You're a good boy. Cooter, take him to the bunkhouse and get him a bed for the night. Tomorrow, I'll take you to town for a haircut and some new clothing."

"That would be wonderful, Mr. Tuttle. I promise to work off every dime."

"That won't be necessary, son, but I'll let you decide. Now, go get some shut-eye, and we'll see you here at first light for some breakfast."

Cooter waited for Rory to finish washing the dishes for Millie, then he opened the kitchen door. "The rain has slowed some, Rory. Let's get on over to the bunkhouse. It's been a while since I've had any company out there." And they both walked out the door and across the large yard.

The bunkhouse was a large cement block building that was a little hard to tell it originally was painted white; Jacob noticed the bunkhouse as well as the main house needed painting badly. And both roofs required repairs, especially with the sometimes rough weather that Tyler gets. This bunkhouse had a pitched shingled roof missing lots of shingles, and the fascia board was in lousy repose.

Cooter had his room by the front door and let Rory pick his bunk, which was many to choose from. At one time, this building housed at least a dozen or more men. But it was kept warm and cozy from a large wood fire fireplace right at the front door with a high chimney that was high above the roof. After a nice shower and a clean shave, he went right to bed and found sleep quickly.

He dreamt of his parents remembering the rodeo circuits and the hotels in the many towns he had visited. Then, as if it had just happened, the highway patrolmen came to his room and told him of his parent's sudden death. He woke up startled and sweating profusely. Cooter was standing by his bunk staring at him.

"Are you okay, son?" handing him a dry towel.

Rory took it, then sat up and wiped his face and neck. "Yes, sir, I guess," his eyes bloodshot and tired.

"Hard thing for you, I'm sure, son. Give yourself some time. It'll get easier." Cooter looked at him with sympathizing eyes. Silence filled the bunkhouse; neither had words to speak. Cooter smiled and went back to shaving in the sink, staring at himself in the mirror. He watched Rory get up and make up his bed in the reflection of the mirror.

After they were both dressed and cleaned, they left the bunkhouse, and the sun was peeping up in the eastern sky as they strolled to the main house. The aroma of bacon and eggs frying along with coffee got their appetite's going.

Rory saw Millie in the kitchen with her apron on and standing by the stove through the window, and he smiled. Cooter grinned watching him. "Son, Mr. Tuttle has turned many a help away from his ranch, and he can see something in you."

Rory smiled, "I won't let him or any of you down, Coot. This I promise." He touched the old man's wrist gently with respect.

John Tuttle carried his grandson into the kitchen and put him in his high chair just as the two ranch hands came into the kitchen and sat down to eat. Millie smiled and commenced to serving all of them their breakfast. John said the blessing, and they ate and talked about the day's events like they were one big family, and Rory felt like he had found his home. John spoke of the ranch and how he had once had hundreds of horses and cattle and a dozen or more ranch hands. The economy and prices caused him to downsize little by little, and the aides had left one by one, finding better jobs around Texas.

Now, he has only fifty or more of each horse and cattle, with twenty thousand or so acres of land. But life managed on, and all was well at the LL Ranch. After breakfast and feeding the stock, John took Rory into Tyler for some new clothes, a haircut, and some new boots, introducing the young man to some friends, and they had lunch with the local sheriff whom John was good friends with.

Several days later, Rory was proving himself to be a right hand at ranching. He was good with the stock and had a stiff back, and this was the combination of a right rancher. And Rory could ride, rope, and shoe the animals. He quickly asked John for paint and had begun painting the house and the bunkhouse and informed them the barns and corrals needed painting as well. He even showed Tuttle and Cooter some tricks his daddy and the man Rider had taught him about caring for the sick animals.

Rory rotated the grazing horses in the front and side yards to keep the grass low and to look mowed, and he supplemented their diets with fresh-cut hay and oats and barley for dessert. The horses moved about slow and content, swatting their tails back and forth, looking happy that someone was here again and caring for them.

He was beginning to feel at home on the LL Ranch, and he didn't mind getting three square meals a day prepared by pretty young women. In the mornings, Millie always had a cup of hot coffee waiting for him in the kitchen; she knew just how he liked it. And when she wasn't cooking or taking care of her son, she would sit on the wooden corrals and watch Rory work without a shirt on, flexing his ripped muscles that covered his stomach and chest.

John Tuttle was away most of the time, buying and selling his stock. He would have mostly semitrucks transporting them back and forth from the ranch; he enjoyed coming home to newly built and freshly painted corrals and two new barns to house them. Rory and Cooter became good friends and thoroughly enjoyed breaking the wild horses and bulls just for the fun of it.

Local ranchers envied John Tuttle, seeing him proper and brag about the new ranch hand he had that was beautifying and bringing new life to the LL Ranch. Months and months of hard work was paying off in a big way for John Tuttle; all of a sudden, he was back in the big time again with interested parties requesting the bred and trained stock that the LL Ranch was breeding and training.

A little over a year and a half later, Rory had asked Millie to marry him. John was thrilled that he was going to have a son-in-law that would take over the ranch for him someday. Rory and Millie had a big wedding, with people from all over Texas that had come to be a part of. Now, Willie had a stepfather that loved him, and Millie was thrilled.

The LL Ranch was a beautiful twenty-thousand-acre spread that had prospered with new animals and new buildings, and they completely remodeled the main house with all modern furnishings. It was so beautiful that the local's living in town would go on week-end drives to visit and see the newly transformed ranch that brought new energy to Tyler, Texas.

Rory had the respect of the family and townspeople alike, see-ing his hard work and good intentions and his devotion to the LL Ranch. He had brought a new beginning to the homestead. One hot afternoon, Rory and Cooter were bathing and grooming some of the young colts that the ranch had spawned when Millie brought them out some ice tea and egg salad sandwiches for lunch. "Are you two handsome men hungry?" she smiled.

"Now, I know that was for your sweetheart." Cooter laughed as he hung a wet towel over the wooden stall.

"Now, Cooter, you're my man too," she kidded.

Rory smiled as he finished brushing down a light brown baby foe and hugged her, whispering a thank you into her ear for being such a good girl. Turning to Millie, he said, "Thank you, honey. I'd love to take a break and eat some." The couple hugged as Cooter smiled and sat down on a bale of hay and drinking some from his glass of tea, watching the two lovebirds. They all sat together, enjoy-ing the warm spring air and just talked about the ranch. Willie was up at the house with the babysitter.

Millie hugged Rory and with a suspicious smile whispered in his ear, getting a big smile and a "What?"

Cooter looked curiously at the two, still trying to give them their privacy. "What's this about? Why the big smiles?"

"Oh, my gosh, Cooter! I'm going to be a father! Whoopee," he yipped and threw his cowboy hat up in the air. He picked up Millie and hugged her.

She looked at Cooter with a smiling face. "Yes, Cooter, I'm pregnant with Rory's baby."

"Well, I'll be. Does your father know?" looking at her.

"He will get home tonight. He called and said he'll be back from Amarillo at seven or so. I'd cook up some steaks and all the fixings and maybe a cake, then we'll tell him together." She looked at Rory, who was washing his sandwich down with some cold tea.

"I think that will be wonderful, honey. I look forward to it. I think another grandson will enlighten and bring him joy."

Cooter hugged Millie.

That evening, John Tuttle was thrilled with the news; he rejoiced and clapped his hands in delight. "I'm so very happy for the two of you!" Tears filled his eyes.

Eight months later, Millie gave birth to a healthy baby boy. Rory had the honor of naming him Jacob John Bramble, giving his middle name after his grandfather Tuttle. Not long after that, a social worker had brought two young girls from the local orphanage in Tyler who knew of the famous quickly growing LL Ranch.

Sarah was eight, and Jenny was five, and they were sisters who had also lost their parents to a fatal car accident, just like Rory. John was to keep them for six months to a year to see how well they adjusted to their new surroundings, and it turned out they loved the family and were a great help to Millie with her two sons.

The girls were young but eager and very loving kids. Rory was delighted and laughed with them and treated them as his own. Cooter and John were so pleased with their family; life was grand again. They were all one big happy family, equally sharing any chores and helping each other. Rory and John had enrolled Sarah and Jenny in school and took turns taking them back and forth into Tyler every day.

Three years later and things were still going wonderfully on the ranch. Rory tended to whatever needed to be done, whether it be mending fences or taking care of the breeding stock, which had multiplied many times over in the more-than-five years he had been on the ranch. John had legally adopted both girls; they had changed their last names to Tuttle. Sarah was now eleven, and Jenny was eight years old, and both were attending school in Tyler.

With the addition of the four new corrals and two large barns that had been added to the ranch, helping to house the ever-increasing stock consisting of more cows and horses. John often bought Brahma bulls to raise and had quite the reputation from the rodeo circuits that were purchasing Tuttle stock for their rodeos. Cowboys from all over the country came to visit the LL Ranch after hearing rumors from John about the late Campbell and Ellie Bramble's son running his ranch. They watched and admired Rory training the bucking bulls for the circuit.

Cooter and Rory gave free classes for young and up-and-coming cowboys who wanted to learn to rope and ride. Millie often became angry with Rory for not charging them fees; Rory refused, always saying that God gave him the LL and a new start, and this was his repayment to help others who loved this sport.

Sarah and Jenny would often take their brothers three-year-old Jacob and six-year-old Willie to watch Rory in the LL arena to watch him ride the bucking bulls and untamed horses. They would laugh and clap their hands together in support of him. Millie somehow seemed to be changing; less and less she allowed her son Willie to be a part of the group with the other children. She had become grumpy and moody at times, often yelling at the girls and little Jacob.

Rory could feel something wasn't right but kept it to himself, not wanting to cause John Tuttle any grief. He had great respect and love for his father-in-law, and he loved him like a he was his birth father, and he felt the same for his best friend and mentor ole Cooter.

Rory also had strong loyalty to Reilly Rider, who was still confined in the Texarkana prison. For the last five years, he made regular visits to the Texarkana prison to visit him and the warden. He would take them young colts and Brahmas for the prison rodeos and donate them and the feed to help other inmates who were trying to rehabilitate themselves.

Rory laughed and kept Rider and the warden updated on the progress of the LL Ranch and his family. The rider felt like Rory was the son he never had and would laugh and giggle at the pictures and stories Rory told him about Jacob and the girls. Rider was so proud of Rory and the life God had given him.

One day, after feeding the stock and cleaning out most of the stalls and hanging the leather tack neatly in their respective places, he looked worried, and Cooter noticed it. "So tell me, Coot, what are your feelings about Millie and me?"

Cooter looked at him and smiled, "What do you mean, son?"

Rory put the rake he was holding against the wooden stall. "Well, have you noticed anything different?"

"Different about Millie?" Cooter wiped the sweat from his brow with his handkerchief and put it back in his back pocket.

"Well, I haven't said anything, but for months now, Millie seems irritable not only with me but with the children as well."

Cooter sat down on a wooden chair and looked at Rory. "Millie has her way, I guess."

"Yes, that she does." Rory sighed and leaned against the wooden stall, staring out in the direction of the southern fields.

"Rory, is there something bothering you?"

"No, I guess not, Cooter."

Cooter stood up and patted Rory on the shoulder. "You know, if there is, you can always tell me, son. I'm a pretty understanding fellow."

Rory smiled, "Yes, you are, Coot."

"Son, you're a good boy, and you come from good stock. Why, the things Mr. Tuttle told me about Campbell and Ellie Bramble, well, I can see their good traits in you. And you'll pass them on to your son Jacob and the girls." He picked up a pail full of oats and let one of the baby calves eat from it.

Rory smiled. "Thanks, pal. I loved my parents. When they died, I guess a little of myself died with them. When I got mixed up with those bad kids in the orphanage, I was full of apathy and anger in my heart. I needed to be accepted by my peers, and I just wanted to belong," he sighed, tears filling his eyes.

Cooter patted him on the shoulder. "I know, son. I know how tough it can be. But I feel I should warn you about Millie. She had always wanted off of her father's ranch. Been that way before you ever came here. You're kind and honest, Rory, but she's not you."

Rory spoke, "The other day, I was telling her how lucky we are to be here and how this is a great place to raise a child."

Cooter looked at him. "Yes."

"Well, she got angry and accused me of not loving Willie. She said I was partial to Jacob and the girls, and it came out of nowhere." Rory closed the gate on their corral.

"Have you said anything to Mr. Tuttle?"

"No, sir. I don't want to cause any problems for him. He has been like a father to me, and I love him."

Cooter smiled. "Well, just hang in there. Maybe it's just a passing moment for her."

"I hope so, Coot. Those kids have got a long way to go yet."

Then they both walked away toward the barn to stack some bales of hay from the truck shipment that had come just hours earlier. As they worked together putting the hay bales in place in the barn, Rory thought of Millie and Jacob. His son's mother was sinking deeper into a depression, and that bothered him. He couldn't understand why. The LL Ranch was a great home, and they had a great family. He smiled again and murmured to himself, "Life is still good!"

Rory was still determined to stay on at the LL Ranch and raise his son while at the same time be a father figure and a good influence on young Jenny and Sarah. His heart was sad for Willie; he wanted to be close with him, but Millie regularly intervened and caused trouble, and he felt Willie was following in her path of discontent and unhappiness. John Tuttle seemed unaware of the problem his daughter was causing everyone and probably for the best. He was getting older, and his heart was weak but in good spirit. Doctors were warning him to quit working so hard and enjoy the good fruits of his hard work at the LL.

Rory, Cooter, and the girls continued to work hard keeping the ranch running smoothly and efficiently, and this kept John happy. They had even hired three new ranch hands to help keep up with the demand. Cooter made it a special event anytime Rory was busting a new bronco or a bull. The girls would laugh and hold little Jacob up on the wooden fencing so he could watch his father, whom he adored in every way.

John consistently made proper money raising and breeding stock; the Texas rodeo circuit officials often relied on him to try out the meanest broncos and Brahma bulls. Rory had become so good at it, he was asked by many of the officials to join the circuit and be a competitor, but he had no desire to leave the LL and his beloved family.

The family had many good times and holidays living on the ranch. They often would take a joyride all together into Tyler, and they were very well known in town as well as in the stockyards with buyers coming from all across the country to buy Tuttle's well-groomed stock.

Jacob attended school in Tyler starting in kindergarten; it was always Rory or Cooter that drove him in town, and sometimes when John was home, he would volunteer to take him. When he was seven years old and in the second grade, he had made friends with a girl he sat next to named Maryann; he would come home and talk about her all the time.

On Sunday mornings, the family would attend the local Assemblies of God church where the girls had joined the choir to sing and worship the Lord. John and Rory always gave a lot in the offering plate and complimented the preacher on his beautiful sermons. He would always tell Cooter and Rory it was a good thing to thank the Lord for all his heavenly blessings bestowed on their family.

Jacob grew to be a good boy and had a great love for the LL and his family. He never seemed to let it bother him that Willie and his mother avoided him and kept to themselves. He was always pleased with his caring sisters and his father, and grandpa and Ole Cooter and Maryann were his world as far as his fourteen years on this earth had counted.

But it almost changed when Maryann was diagnosed with brain cancer; Jacob cried and prayed for her. When he went to church, he would ask the church for a special prayer for his best friend; he loved her very much. And when the doctors told her parents she was terminal, but there was a slight chance if she had surgery on the left side of her brain, Jacob insisted on going to the hospital in Tyler to stay by her hand in her room.

After she had come out from the surgery operation, he wanted to stay in her room with her, but the hospital had rules that children under the age of sixteen had to leave by eight o'clock at night, so he talked his dad into staying with him, and the hospital said okay as long as an adult was with him.

Rory and Jacob would visit her, staying late at night by her side with her family members, waiting for her to recover. Both of them encouraged her and her family with hope. Rory and John gave her parents money to help with the ever-increasing associated bills. Jacob had bought her a unique hat after her hair began falling out after the chemotherapy treatments that she had to have. He sat with her month after month and started to get acquainted with other cancer patients.

CHAPTER 3

One year later, she had made a full recovery, and the doctors said she was in complete remission with her cancer. Other than the medications she had to continue to take, she was allowed to go home again finally and could go back to school in Tyler.

Jacob started to get back into the business of ranching again, and between his father, grandfather, and Cooter, he had reached the very best education a rancher could get. His understanding and training with all animals were impeccable, and he was very loyal and obedient to his family. He loved his mother and brother Willie, even though he could sense they didn't feel the same way about him; there was always some resentment from them, knowing how much the family loved him more than his brother.

When Jacob had turned fifteen, his grandpa John Tuttle went to be with the Lord. The death of his grandfather was a sorrowful time for everyone. His wish was to be buried out in the lower pasture where Millie and Rory had been married under large shade trees. Rory had invited the sheriff and his family, who for many years was a close friend and a brother to John.

In his will, he had left everyone, including Cooter, part of the ranch and land. But most went to Rory and Jacob for the love and strength they had brought back to the LL Ranch. Millie and Willie had become even more resentful after the reading of the will from the lawyer who had represented her father, and her feelings grew worse toward everyone, even the innocent girls.

Time passed along, and Sarah had graduated from Texas A&M with her master's degree in education, and Jenny was working on the same. Both wanted to teach in school, and they were great sisters helping Willie and Jacob with their studies.

The ranch was self-sustainable with various strategically placed water wells and solar heating and electricity. They grew their vegetables and had also begun developing and producing mass quantities of wheat. Rory and Cooter had to hire several more ranch hands, now having a total of eight men to keep up with the demand. Texas A&M University would send summer interns to the ranch who were trying for degrees in agriculture and farming.

The ranch continued to prosper under Rory's influence and charm; he had even been asked by the townspeople in Tyler to run for mayor, of which he smiled and said, "I'm a rancher and family man, not a politician."

Many times Rory and Jacob would saddle up Jacob's bay and Rory's roan horses and spend quiet moments together, riding the twenty-five thousand acres of rangeland and talk about things. Jacob told his dad, "An older kid at school was bullying me, so I punched him."

"I don't condone fighting, son, but I also believe in defending yourself."

His horse blew air through its nostrils and shook its head to keep the flies off of him.

"I know. I'm sorry."

"It's okay, Jacob. You defended yourself."

"This one guy is struck on Maryann, and he had asked her to the prom last week, and she had told him no, so he picked a fight with me."

"I see." Rory grinned as he gazed around the area they rode in.

"I don't think he will bother me again. Maryann's older brother, who is in his grade, beat him up for picking a fight with me"—looking at his dad for a reaction.

Rory said, "So her brother defended you?"

"Well, yes, but he had another reason as well"—glancing toward Rory.

"Did he say why, son?"—returning the glance.

"The guy wanted Maryann, and her brother worried about her. That guy was calling him names to hurt Maryann and me."

Rory looked at him. "I guess her brother showed him, huh? Doesn't she have four brothers?"

"Yes, she has three older and one younger brother." He gently guided his horse around a big, vast pit in the ground.

"Well, Jacob, I don't judge anyone. I leave that to God. He stood up for his sister and you. That says what his character is, and I like him."

"I do too, Dad. He's a great person!"

Jacob worshiped his father; he would ask him questions about life in general and relish the answers his dad would give him. Rory loved his son and had always tried to do right by him; he felt that Jacob needed to know his roots and told him all the stories of what his life had been with Ellie and Campbell Bramble.

They believed in God and were great followers and supporters of the Martin Luther King peace movement, giving to him in any way they could. The good Lord and America had meant much to them, and they wanted to give back to all they could.

They spent many hours together riding or walking their horses through the tall blowing wheat and tall grass out on the lower ridge. Sometimes they just listened to the gentle wind blowing and gazing at times into the beautiful Tyler, Texas, skies. Rory honored his parents' memories and told his son what his life was like and how he had spent time in prison.

Tyler was a beautiful place to live and raise a family, except for an occasional thunderstorm or maybe even a tornado that sometimes passed through. Rory would tell Jacob some history of Texas that John Tuttle had told him, like the two worst that was in Waco, Texas, on May 11, 1953, and the other was in Goliad, Texas, that happened on May 22, 1902. Both storms devastated over a hundred people. "Ranchers need to know the weather. Their livelihood as ranchers depended on it," he told his son.

Rory told Jacob about the Alamo, as what John Tuttle had told him many times, and how true Texans knew that the real story was never known because there were no survivors. The stories were put together through the years after Mexicans who were there told their versions of what they saw and heard. Like Davy Crockett's body was rumored to have been found by the south wall gate; how he died, no one will ever know.

What people did know was that less than two hundred or so brave men gave their lives against thousands of Mexico's General Santa Anna's soldiers to help buy more time when they thought General Sam Houston was coming to their aid.

As they continued to walk, Jacob would always watch his dad adhere to his surroundings, listening to their horses blow air through their nostrils and sometimes shake their heads to keep the flies away, and the sound of the hackamores in their mouths make clacking sounds. "Dad, what are some of the things you look for when you're buying new stock?"

Rory smiled and thought for a second. "Well, son, when you first talk to the owner, look at the man selling the stock. What kind of a person is he or she? How do they care for their stock?"

"Okay," Jacob answered.

"Then, you listen to hear what they have to say about the stock they are trying to unload. When the people are done talking, you think about everything that was said and everything not mentioned about the stock." Rory smiled.

"What else, Dad?" Jacob questioned.

"Well, you look for signs of disease. You look for diarrhea. Colic is another issue. It usually is caused by feeding errors and can lead to intestinal parasites." He continued, "There are respiratory problems like influenza and bronchial asthma, and don't forget the foot and leg problems."

Jacob smiled at his dad. "Boy, you sure know a lot, Dad! I hope someday I'll be as good as you." He patted his bay on the side of its neck.

"Jacob, someday you'll be much better and smarter than your old dad. Every father dreams that his children will be much better than they were. I love all of my kids. You, Willie, Sarah, and Jenny."

"I know you do, Dad! We love you too!"

Rory smiled and turned his strawberry roan around toward which they had come, and Jacob followed. "Come on, son. Let's get back home. It's near to supper time."

"I'll race you, Dad!" And Jacob took off in a lope with his father coming up behind him, and they ran the horses most of the way home. Rory smiled, watching his son in the saddle ahead of him.

The next day, Rory had taken sixteen-year-old Jacob with him into Tyler; the stockyard proprietor had called Rory about an ailing Brahma that had delivered its baby only weeks earlier. The man wanted to put the mother out of her misery, but the baby had not been weaned from her yet.

He had called the LL and wanted Rory to take both of them, knowing she may have a fighting chance in the care of the Brambles. Jacob stood and watched his dad look at the mother and baby in their stall; he examined her in a careful, humane way along with the veterinarian on site. Then he studied the baby and came back out of the booth.

In talking with the stockyard proprietor, he told him the mother was too far gone, and the baby probably wouldn't make it without proper hand-feeding and antibiotics to strengthen him. So the proprietor decided just to put both of them down; he did not want to put any more expense in them.

Two hours later, Rory and Jacob had gotten help to load the baby into their truck trailer. Rory had struck a deal to take the baby home and try and save his life; the mother had to be put down. Jacob watched his dad pay the proprietor and the veterinarian a significant amount of money to help them cover the cost of their lost expenses; the veterinarian was to come out to the LL Ranch twice a week and give medicine to the baby.

"Dad, this baby Brahma doesn't look too good," Jacob commented.

Rory smiled with confidence. "I remember a young man who arrived almost twenty years ago to the LL Ranch. He was scared, hungry, and almost fainted. But he was tough and determined. A kind man named John Tuttle gave him a chance and a new life!"

Jacob smiled. "That was you, Dad."

"Son, this Brahma is for you, and we will call him Tuff Bramble for all our hardships. I know the good Lord has a reason for us being called here today. My faith tells me there is a life I can save." He patted Jacob on the arm as he closed the gate to the trailer.

"You're giving me this Brahma?"

"I sure am! I sure am! Let's go home, son." They drove back some twenty miles to the LL Ranch, and Rory got a few of the ranch hands to help them physically pick up the Brahma and carry him into the barn and put him in his clean new hay-filled bed.

The baby was so weak, it could not even stand on its own, and from that moment on, they hand-fed and cleaned and talked the Brahma to health. With the veterinarian coming and giving antibiotics, the baby got better and grew and grew. Rory and Jacob took on the task of saving this baby's life, even against the wishes of Millie, who complained they spent too much time with him.

Jacob took on the responsibility of checking on him before school, and after football practice, he came home and took care of Tuff while still doing the daily chores that his uncle Cooter had assigned him. Rory went about his duties on the ranch, allowing Jacob some freedom from the breaking of bulls and untamed horses so he could take care of his pet Brahma.

It tickled Rory's heart that Jacob was just like him and his father Campbell; they had great compassion for animals. They never mistreated the wild ones that came to the LL for breaking and taming; they patiently gave love and understanding to them. They would humanely saddle break them so even a little child could ride them.

Still, Rory's heart ached for Willie and his wife that seemed to resent Jacob. He was so proud of his girls who had the desire for higher learning and yearned to stay with the ranch even though they could have left with all of their education and went about their lives. Ranching was a tough life for most; it took a particular breed of people.

Rory was hoping Jacob would go on to college as well. It seemed Willie did not like school and spent most of his time with his mother frequenting Tyler's local bars and clubs. Several times, Cooter and he had to bail them out of jail.

After several years, the baby Brahma Tuff had grown into a beautiful eighteen-hundred-pound adult bull. He was more of a pet instead of a bucking beast, having been hand-fed and bathed regularly and talked to like he was human. People would say that he would respond also and smile like he was their child; Jacob and the ranch hands were much to blame. Jacob would often bring home his football buddies to play with Tuff.

At eighteen years old, Jacob had perfect grades in school and was the star quarterback on the football team with credit for leading them to the divisional championship title. He much loved his long-time girlfriend Maryann, who was always very supportive of him. He often laughed when talking with his dad that he hated math and science, but his two sisters had bullied him into learning them.

As graduation grew closer, Jacob was being groomed by scouts in colleges around the country for his quarterbacking skills; Sarah and Jenny would do his bidding for him. They protected and loved him and insisted the scouts come and talk with them, and they watched for aggressive agents that might have their best interest in mind and not their brother's, who were an all-around athlete and scholar.

One week before his high school graduation, Jacob had come home and seen an ambulance driving away from the ranch. In a panic, he ran to the front house and found Sarah and Jenny crying.

"What happened? What's wrong, sisters," he asked with a weird look on his face.

Sarah stopped crying, stood up, and hugged him, then looked in his eyes. "Jacob, Dad died over by the corrals a couple of hours ago. Cooter is distraught and is down in the bunkhouse with some of the hands that found him."

"What?" he burst into tears. "No! Not dad!"

Jenny stood up and hugged him. "Oh, Jacob, honey! Cooter said he had just gotten off of one of the red mares he was saddle breaking. Several of the hands that were helping him said he just dismounted and fell on the ground clutching his chest. One of them ran and got Cooter to help. By the time the ambulance got here from the town, he was already gone. The county coroner came out and pronounced him dead, and the ambulance just took him away."

Jacob sat down on the front steps, putting both hands over his face and bawled a pitiful cry. "My dad is gone? Why God? Why?" he sobbed.

Maryann had arrived, and with Sarah and Jenny, they tried their best to comfort him, and together they sat on the porch for an hour. "Where are Mom and Willie?" Jacob asked.

"We don't know, honey. The sheriff is trying to find them to tell them. Who knows?" Sarah spoke in a quiet voice.

Jacob hugged all of them and walked down to the barn and spent the rest of the evening with Tuff and Cooter. They grieved together, and Cooter attempted to talk things out with him. The ranch hands gave him all the help they could, assuring him and Cooter they were sorry they could not have done more to help; they had loved him as well!

Several days later, they had a funeral down in the lower pasture and buried Rory next to John Tuttle and his wife. Most everyone who knew him attended, except Millie and Willie; this was an appropriate thing Cooter had explained to all of them. After the funeral, Jacob stayed behind by his father's grave site all day and into the evening. Cooter and the ranch hands attended to the daily chores, understanding the boy's feelings.

Having stayed up all night, Jacob slept in the next day. After getting up and dressed, he walked down to Tuff's stall, wanting to see him and talk for a while. When he arrived, he found the stall gate open, and Tuff was nowhere to be found. "What? Someone help me!" Hysterically, he ran around the barn, looking and screaming for Tuff. The ranch hands ran to him, wondering why he was crying.

"Jacob, what's wrong?" Cooter yelled at him.

"Where's Tuff, Cooter?" he screamed hysterically. "I can't find him."

"Well, I don't know. Did any of you see Tuff?" he asked the hands.

No one spoke until one of them spoke up. "You know, come to think of it, early this morning, I had come out of the bunkhouse and saw the Tyler stockyard truck pulling a trailer, and it was pretty far up the road. I didn't think much of it being so early in the morning."

Cooter looked at Jacob. "Get the truck, son. We'll go find out what is going on here."

An hour later, they arrived at the stockyards and talked with the proprietor. "Why was your truck at the LL Ranch early this morning?"

"Well, we were there to pick up that Brahma Millie sold to us yesterday. Why do you ask?"

Jacob screamed and grabbed the man by his shirt collar. "That was my bull, mister. I didn't sell him."

The man pulled away in a frenzy, and Cooter grabbed Jacob's hand that was going to hit the man. "Mister, you had no right to take that bull," Cooter told him.

"Cooter, I have a bill of sale right here"—pulling a piece of paper out of his pocket. "I paid twenty thousand dollars for that prize Brahma." He took a breath. "Signed right here by Millie Bramble."

"He wasn't hers to sell, mister," Jacob screamed at him. "That was me and my dad's bull. We raised him from a baby."

Cooter looked at the man. "This boy's father died a week ago, and that bull was their pet."

"Well, I'm sorry, son. I didn't know. Millie came here with a young man and wanted to sell him. I got a spanking deal."

"Where's he at. I'll repurchase him right now!" Cooter told him.

The man wiped his mouth with his handkerchief. "He's not here, and I sold him to a man named Jim Rogers for more than I paid. He loaded him up and took him away. I don't know where he went."

Jacob started crying and turned away. "First my dad and now Tuff? What is going on here?"

Cooter looked at the man. "Do you know what you've done, mister?"

"I'm sorry. That's all a man can say, son"—seeing Jacob was crying. "If I had known this, I never would have bought that bull. That lady didn't tell me any of this."

Jacob continued to cry on Cooter's shoulder, and Cooter held his head. "That bull was part of our family, mister."

They stood for some time together until Jacob was able to stop crying, and the man offered some help. "Well, let me see. I do know the man's name, and I know he spends time in Fort Worth and

Amarillo, Texas. He buys for the pro rodeo circuit. If I miss my guess, that bull is intended to ride the circuit. There's only one pro circuit, son. You might be able to track him down. Might be hard, but you might do it."

Cooter and Jacob looked at him and thought for a second. "Mister, we're not happy with you right now, but I offer my apology. This boy is a good boy."

The man shook his hand. "I can see that."

The two got in their truck and drove back home to make a plan of action. "I've no good words for my mom and my brother," Jacob said quietly, and Cooter kept driving in silence.

Back at the ranch and sitting at the dinner table, Jacob sat quietly, stirring his food with his fork but not eating. "Jacob, you need nourishment, honey," Jenny told him.

"I looked in Mom and Willie's room, Cooter, and they are gone, baggage and all," Sarah spoke up. "I haven't seen them since the funeral."

"They probably cleaned out her bank accounts too. Good thing Grandpa Tuttle and Rory never allowed her access to the ranch accounts. Her dad knew she would do this one day," Cooter added.

There was a knock at the front door, and the door opened, and Maryann had come to check on Jacob. "Hi, everyone. I couldn't stay home."

Jacob stood up and pulled a chair at the dinner table for her. "Hi Mary." He looked sad.

Minutes later, another knock and the door opened, and it was Sarah's boyfriend Deputy Sherriff Luke Naylor. "Hi, everyone." He was not in uniform.

"Hi, Luke," Sarah spoke up. "Will you two join us for supper?"

"Well, I didn't come here for that, but I am hungry," he answered. Luke was a thirty-six-year-old, honest, and upright law officer and had been dating Sarah for two years or more. Sitting down to the dinner table and putting his napkin across his lap, he said, "Cooter, I stopped at the stockyard in Tyler and talked with the manager. He confirmed what you told me that Millie and her son offered him a good price for Tuff, and he, in turn, sold him to a rodeo circuit promoter. The promoter buys and sells animals all around Texas"—looking sadly at Jacob.

"Thank you, Luke! I appreciate all the help," Jacob responded.

"You're welcome, Jacob," Luke answered.

The kitchen table was quiet for a while as everyone silently ate their food. Jacob thought about what he was going to do, knowing he had to participate in the graduation from high school, even if just for his dad, who was so very proud of him. He'd received many offers from different colleges to attend and had been offered full-ride scholarships to play football as a promising quarterback.

After dinner, Luke Naylor kissed Sarah goodbye and drove away down the long rode out of the ranch property. While the others went about the evening chores, Jacob and Maryann sat quietly at the living room desk his dad had bought just a year ago; they talked together about what he must do. All he could think about was Tuff and his dad.

Later, Sarah, Jenny, and Cooter came into the living room study, seeing Jacob and Maryann sitting in the dimly lit room just staring at the family Bible. The girls sat down next to them as Cooter stood by Rory's bookshelf, thumbing through the selection of books he used to like to read, being he was an avid reader.

CHAPTER 4

Jacob held a framed picture of Tuff and him and his dad standing in his barn, bathing Tuff when he was a baby. He thought of the two cute pure-white star-shaped markings located on tuffs face and nose, something that tickled his dad when they first saw him, and he managed a smile.

Jenny reached out and rubbed Jacobs's shoulder. "Jacob, if there's anything we can do for you, please tell us."

"Thanks. I love you, guys, but I think I want to be alone right now." He turned to Maryann.

"Okay." She kissed him on the forehead. "Sure, Jacob. I'll see you tomorrow at school, okay?"

"Sure." He managed a smile. "I have to pray and ask God what he wants me to do. I think I'll sit here a while, if you guys don't mind."

They had never seen him so sad before in his whole life. They all walked away, but before leaving the room, Cooter looked at him with watery eyes. He thought about Rory and John Tuttle, and now his boy was all alone to deal with his thoughts, and he left the room with the girls.

In the kitchen, Jenny looked at Sarah and Cooter. "I've just had it with Millie and Willie."

Sarah spoke up, "Jenny, we don't know for sure any of this is true yet. Let Luke investigate the facts."

Jenny blurted out with tears in her eyes, "They've done some pretty bad things over the years, and you know it. You know darn good and well that she did this. She's been trying for years to get

Willie in Hollywood to become an actor, and he doesn't have a talented bone in his body."

"Girls, all right now. The truth will come out. It always does in the end. Everything will work out the way it's supposed to!" Cooter replied calmly as a sixty-nine-year-old man would do.

Days later into the next week, Jacob and Maryann had finished their graduation from high school, and they were having a big celebration with both families at the ranch. Maryann's family and friends had joined in with the Brambles. There were even scouts from several colleges there trying to get around Sarah and Jenny to recruit Jacob for their athletics programs.

Ole Cooter quieted everyone for a toast of lemonade for the young graduates. "Listen up, everyone." The crowd grew quiet. "I want to toast Jacob and Maryann for their hard work and dedication to their studies. Both of them maintained a perfect 4.0 grade average, which is superb!" And everyone raised their glasses and cheered them.

Then Sheriff Luke Naylor spoke up, "I have an announcement as well. Sarah and I are going to be married in October this fall!" He raised his glass, and everyone followed with praises for them.

"That's wonderful, Luke and Sarah!" Jacob hugged both of them. "I've always liked you, Luke, and so did my dad."

"Thank you, Jacob!" Luke and Sarah told him.

Cooter walked up to them. "Congratulations, kids! I figured it wouldn't be long. I'm so happy for you two." He shook hands with Luke and hugged Sarah.

"Thank you, Cooter!" Sarah smiled, grasping ahold of Luke's hand with her own. "We plan on staying on with the ranch, if that's okay?" Sarah asked.

"Of course it is. We couldn't get by without you." Cooter grinned.

Luke spoke up, "Sarah will be teaching in Tyler, and I'll keep my job as sheriff's deputy. But we want to stay on and help out all we can when at home."

"That's great, you two." Jacob smiled as he held on to Maryann's hand. "I have an announcement to make to." Everyone stopped to hear him talk. "I have decided that the college will have to wait for now."

"What?" people were saying to each other.

Maryann looked at him with a surprised gasp. "What, Jacob?"

"I have decided that I need to go find Tuff. I'm going to track him down and bring him home."

"Jacob, why didn't you tell me?" Maryann asked with tears in her eyes.

He gazed into her eyes. "Mary, I could take the easy way out and go to college with some scholarships and play ball and forget all about Tuff and my dad, who is gone now. I'd have the scouts and the coaches wanting me to play football for them. But if I don't do this, I'll be sorry for the rest of my life. Right now, at this very moment, Tuff is probably wondering where he is and why he was taken from us. His whole world has been changed because of my mother."

Everyone gasped and listened to Jacob talk. "My dad and I brought him home when he was a baby, and his mother had to be put to sleep. What if someone is mistreating him? Oh no. I won't allow that to happen to him. I'm out of school now. Luke will be living here and helping out. I'm going, and that's that."

Maryann cried, "Well, we both have scholarships to Texas A&M. I can't go without you, Jacob. You're my best friend in the whole world, so I'm not going either. I'm going with you." She sobbed with tears coming out of her eyes. "I'm going wherever you go."

Jenny blurted out, "I'm going with you too, little brother, and you need me to help you."

Jacob smiled and looked at her. "No, you're not, either of you. This is something I have to do myself—for my dad and me. Maryann, you're going to be a doctor. Remember what you went through and the doctors and surgeons that saved you and all that we talked about? You're a gifted person, and you have God-given talent for helping people. All our teachers told you that." He kissed her. "This country needs good doctors like you, honey! I would not take that from you. I want you to go without me. I promise I'll be back. I promise." And he walked away with her up to the house, and they went inside.

The college scouts tried to talk with the girls and Cooter to talk him out of this nonsense, but they said no. These events changed the whole atmosphere of the party, and the crowds spoke for a while and slowly began to leave and go home, and Cooter made sure the ranch hands had eaten and went back to work, taking care of the animals and the ranch.

The next morning came fast, and Jenny came running into the kitchen where Sarah and Cooter were having breakfast. "Jacob's gone, and he left a note. It reads, 'Dearest family, I couldn't sleep last night, so I just decided to go. Forgive me for not saying goodbye, but I was eager to hit the road to find Tuff…I'm taking my dad's truck, and I'll either write or call you soon. Love, Jacob.'"

"Well, he meant what he said yesterday. May the Lord be with him," Cooter spoke out.

Sarah cried, "I hope he'll be okay. He's never been alone before, and this world can be cruel and mean to a young person."

Cooter watched the two girls cry. "Girls, that boy will be fine, and a man feels a tugging inside him at some point in his life. It's all a part of who he will become. He knows we're here for him, and the good Lord will protect him."

At that very moment, Jacob had stopped his truck at the stockyard in Tyler and talked with the manager. He found out the rodeo promoter's name was Jim Rogers, and the last anyone heard, he had headed for Amarillo for that next rodeo.

He found out that Rogers travels around Texas and Arizona, booking acts for his show, so Jacob headed for Amarillo, driving his dad's truck with great courage and determination to save Tuff. He remembered the stories his father and grandfather had told him of how the Brambles had struggled for years, chasing the circuit to earn a meager living. A lump formed in his throat, thinking Jim Rogers might have gone to Fort Worth. Still, he drove the nine-hour trip to Amarillo without stopping to rest. Suddenly, fear came upon him, and he felt homesick for his family.

He parked his truck by some corrals and got out spitting on the ground, and he wiped his watering eyes. "Gosh dang it! I'm a Bramble, and we come by life the hard way. I have to make good on

my life, and it will even the score for my dad and my grandparents."
Suddenly, he received strength and went on walking to find Tuff.

He looked in every stall he could find for over an hour, and the evening had surrounded him. A big burly man approached him. The man had a beard that covered his face and clothing that looked worn and not new. "Howdy, son! What are you looking for? I saw you looking around here."

A little apprehensive talking with this big man, who kind of frightened him. "I'm looking for my dad's Brahma bull."

Rubbing his chin, he replied, "What makes you think he's here?"

"I was told a man named Jim Rogers might have brought him here, but I'm not sure, honestly." Jacob sized the man up compared to his six foot one inch and 190 pounds of himself.

"I know Jim Rogers. I don't know if he's in town today. I could go check. Are you sure he brought your dad's bull here?"

Jacob was tired as it had been a long day, and he didn't sleep the night before. He answered slowly, "No sir, I'm not. I was hoping—" He felt like crying and turned away to hide it.

"Are you all right, son?" seeing the boy had emotions.

"You see, Rogers bought my dad's bull from the stockyards in Tyler. They had purchased him illegally from my mother while I was at my dad's funeral, and I want him back." He felt dizzy from not eating all day.

The big fellow looked concerned at hearing the story. "I'm sorry, son. By the way, my name is Buck Thompson, and I take care of all the stock that comes through here. I haven't seen any Brahmas in several weeks."

"I'm Jacob Bramble from the LL Ranch in Tyler. I want to thank you for your help." Feeling defeated and exhausted, he turned to walk back to his truck.

Buck finished pouring oats to his stock and yelled out to him, "Jacob, come back. I might be able to help you."

Jacob stopped in his tracks and walked back to the man. "So, how can you help me, Buck?"

"When you said your name, I was curious. What was your father's name?" He sat down his bucket and looked at the boy.

"Rory Bramble."

The man smiled and patted Jacob on the shoulder. "I thought so, and I knew your dad very well. Once upon a time."

Jacob smiled. "You did, Buck?"

"You bet I did! We were in the Texarkana prison together." Then he stopped smiling. "Rory passed on?"

"Yes. Two weeks ago in Tyler. The doctor said he had a heart attack." His eyes were red.

Buck looked at Jacob, noticing he looked tired. Sadly, he said, "I'm sorry to hear that. Rory Bramble was my friend. You see, there were three of us that stuck together in prison a long time ago. Your Dad and I and a man named Reilly Rider, the famous rodeo man."

Suddenly Jacob remembered the stories. "Yes, you're Buck Thompson. My dad told me about you guys." He smiled and shook hands.

Buck scratched his chin and looked lost in thought for a second. "I'll tell you what, Jacob. Can you stay on for a couple of days until I can make some contacts? I might be able to help you for old times' sake!" he smiled.

Hesitating for a second. "Where would I stay, Buck?"

"You can stay in our fifth-wheel trailer over by the arena. There's a guest room all made up. I'll get my wife, Angie, to rustle us up some supper, son. She's a great cook!"

"I could sure eat some and do for some sleep." He looked at Buck. "All right then. It's a deal!" And they shook hands. "I have some money to pay you, Buck."

Buck grinned. "Your money's no good here. My wife runs the restaurant next to the arena, and she will feed you all you want. If you want, tomorrow you can clean and feed the stock as I do. I'll make some phone calls, and we'll see what happens."

Jacob walked back to his truck and got his gear and took it over to the trailer for the night; it was getting dark now. He put his belongings away and met Buck in the restaurant where he introduced Angie to Jacob, and they all sat together and ate dinner.

The next day, after a good night's sleep, they ate breakfast together again, and Jacob returned to the corrals to clean and feed the stock while Buck was away, trying to get information for him. Jacob fed and watered all of the stock consisting of horses and mules and cows, and then he raked and shoveled manure into a wheelbarrow and hauled it to a large trash container and emptied it, then went back and did this stall by stall most of the day.

Around four o'clock, he stopped to watch a broncobuster in the arena area try and ride some rough horses, and he kept getting thrown off, and he landed in the dirt. Jacob caught himself smiling as he watched the guy get repeatedly thrown. Naturally, he saw the mistakes the guy was making as he had been taught by the best—his dad, his grandfather, and Ole Cooter. He noticed this rider was making the silliest mistakes, and it amused him. What he didn't like was the man hit and cussed the horse.

Jacob did not know he was watching Ty Herder, a reigning rodeo up-and-comer. He couldn't help himself from yelling out some advice to the guy. "Hey, mister, try showing that horse some kindness and move your legs with the rhythm of the mustang. Loosen up a bit and stop touching the horse with your free hand, and you'll do fine!"

Ty Herder gave Jacob a mean look and yelled at his assistant who was trying to help him. "You stupid idiot! I told you to hold this animal until I'm ready."

Jacob noticed the young man was a young Native American kid of about twenty or so. The kid just hung his head and complied with the rider, and Jacob went back to shoveling.

Again the bronco came bucking out of the stall and threw the rider off again, and Jacob looked up and laughed. Ty stood up when he saw Jacob laughing at him as he raked manure and yelled out, "Shut up, punk. Do you think you can do better? Stop shoveling that crap and come and try, hotshot!"

Jacob continued to rake and ignored him. Ty Herder walked over to the stall and climbed up on the rails. "I'd say that job suits you just right."

Jacob showed some irritation and looked at him. "A man has no shame in caring for his animals. I'm right happy to help my new friend Buck Thompson." Then he went back to raking.

Ty laughed out loud. "Buck Thompson? Why that fat old has-been. He can't even ride." He was laughing again.

Jacob wheeled the cart over and dumped it by the bin and spoke out. "I think he's a good man, mister."

"Do you know who I am, punk?"

Jacob stopped and took a look at him, then went back to work. "No, but I see you have no respect for God's animals."

"Well listen, kid, I saw you laughing at me. Nobody laughs at Ty Herder!" he seemed to become angrier by the second at Jacob's calm demeanor.

"I'm sorry I offended you. I'll mind my own business."

Ty turned to the boy he was yelling at. "Well, do you hear that? He's sorry." The kid looked the other way, not wanting trouble. "You're not getting off that easy. Stop that shoveling crap and go get on that bronco! Let's see if you can do better."

Feeling a bit angered at Ty, Jacob looked over at the launching gate and saw the kid watching him, then looked back at Ty. "All right, I'll get on board."

Together, Ty and Jacob walked over to the launching gate. Jacob pulled his hat down tight on his head and checked the fit of his gloves. Then he climbed up and over the stall, preparing to seat himself on the restless horse the young Indian was holding for him.

Slowly, he lowered himself down on the animal as he talked to him gently in his ear and calmly patted his neck. And before Jacob was ready, Ty opened the gate and yelled, "Hee-haw!" and out leaped the horse for all it's worth. His assistant glared at him with a sullen look.

Jacob held on as the horse bucked and twisted with all its might, and try as he did, the animal could not throw him off. With one hand, he held the reins, and with a much proactive edge, he sat up straight and began to move his legs in rhythmic and graceful movements.

The horse bucked and leaped into the air; Jacob rode him and didn't let go. After about ten seconds, he reached around and removed the tight leather strap binding the mustang, and he stopped bucking. Jacob rode the bronco back to the stall and jumped off with grace and respect for the animal. He thanked the horse and rubbed his face gently as he was taught, and the horse seemed to sense his kindness.

About that time, there was clapping from the arena bleachers. Jacob looked up and saw Buck Thompson and another man clapping in congratulations. Jacob walked the horse back to the kid at the stall, who was also clapping in excitement and seeing Ty had already left in disgust.

Buck stood up when Jacob arrived. "Jacob, I found the man you are looking for. This is Jim Rogers, the rodeo promoter. He just happened to be around, and I told him about you."

They shook hands. "Pleased to meet you, sir. I'm Jacob Bramble."

Jim smiled at him. "So you are, son. Why didn't I see you when I was at the LL Ranch picking up that prize bull?"

"We were burying my father. Later I found out our bull was missing," he answered as he sat down in the bleachers next to the men.

Jim took a breath of air. "The man at the Tyler stockyard sold me the bull and gave me a bill of sale. Told my men it was okay to go pick him up, and we did just that." He wiped his mouth with his handkerchief. "I gave him thirty-five grand for that animal."

Jacob looked at him. "My dad and I would never have sold Tuff. That's his name. We raised him from a sick calf."

Jim pulled out a bill of sale. "I have a receipt right here, son. The Tyler stockyard sells me lots of animals. He said a woman and a boy came to him offering a deal."

"I believe you, mister. Sounds like something my mother and brother would do. I'm not questioning that."

CHAPTER 5

B uck spoke up, "Jacob, have you talked with your mother about this?"

"No. She disappeared with my brother. She's rumored to have gone out to Hollywood to get Willie in the movies. Otherwise, I haven't a clue?"

Buck looked at Jim Rogers. "Jim, where is Tuff now? Do you know?"

"I'm sorry fellas. I sold him to a promoter who handles the national rodeos. He saw the bull was in tip-top prime condition and quickly offered me more than I paid, so I took it. I'm so sorry. Had I known all this, I would not have done it."

"My God! Poor Tuff has been sold three times. Which way did he go? Did he say?" Jacob asked.

Jim thought for a second, then spoke, "I've no idea, son. Whichever direction the pro rodeo circuit follows."

"I'll follow the rodeo circuit, I guess. Leastways, I might have a better chance of finding Tuff."

"You're green to chase to rodeo and too young to be traveling the country alone, son," Jim told him.

"He won't be alone if I can help him. I knew his dad, and I've spent too many years around here. If you have me, Jacob, Angie can handle things here while I'm gone." Buck looked a little uneasy, knowing the boy just met him yesterday.

Jacob thought for a second, then said, "My dad spoke of you, Buck. I do know you. Yes, I'd like you to come along."

Jim spoke up, "Jacob, where did you learn to ride like that at your young age?"

He smiled. "I grew up riding and learning broncos, Jim. No better place to learn than at home with a family that loves you!"

"Well, do you know who just stormed out of the arena?" Jim smiled, looking at the boy.

"No. Just someone practicing, I guess?"

"Jacob, that was Ty Herder. He's an up-and-comer that has won multiple events in the pro circuit, and he wants a world championship."

"I know who he is," Buck spoke up

"Well I'll be. He didn't seem to treat his horse or that kid working for him very well," Jacob answered back.

Jim grinned. "No, he's not known for being a good person. Just a good cowboy." Giving a more serious look towards Jacob, "Son, you outdid him. If you can ride like that, I'd take advantage of your skills."

"What do you mean, Jim?"

Buck interrupted, "Jim used to be involved with the rodeo when he was younger. Nowadays, he just buys and sells the stock for them because he knew the best and had a top-notch reputation in the industry."

Jim blushed a little. "The best way to find your bull would be to join the circuit and compete. I could use my connections to get you started. With what I just saw, you'd be a good hand."

Jacob smiled. "Would Buck here be my assistant?"

Jim smiled. "He'd be your best asset, and I've known him for many years. But to get to the big time, you need to build a reputation first. You would have to start with the smaller rodeos first, and if you do well, we will go to the big deals. Listen, I can make things happen, I'll set up the appointments and register you to each event, and you follow my leads."

Just then, the Indian kid came walking over to them, leading the horse by the reins. Jacob stood up. "What about him?" pointing.

Buck knew him too. "Tom, do you have a second to talk?"

Jacob shook his hand. "I'm Jacob Bramble."

Tom looked surprised. "Any relation to the famous Campbell Bramble?"

"He was my grandfather."

"Well, I'll be"—taking a moment—"I've heard stories about how he was good to my people through the years."

Jacob smiled. "Where are you from, Tom?"

"I am from the Choctaw Indian reservation in Oklahoma."

Jim Rogers looked at Jacob. "You're kin to Campbell Bramble? I didn't put that together. I never met him but heard many stories that he was the greatest rodeo cowboy that ever lived. Well, I'll be." He shook Jacobs's hand.

"Tom, do you work for Ty Herder?"

"No, Jacob, I work here sometimes, and he just wanted my help today. Why?"

"I'm going to join the circuit to find my Brahma bull Tuff, and if you want, I'd love to have you and Buck here on my team. I don't know how I'd pay you right now. I do have a thousand dollars in my duffle bag to get us started, though."

Buck smiled and looked at Tom. "Best offer I've had in years, Tom. What you say?"

Jim spoke up, "Fellas, one thing I want to warn you about is the treatment of animals."

"What do you mean, Jim? Are you referring to the way Ty treated his horse?" Tom asked.

"Yes. The thing about rodeos is that not all people treat animals good. Some men are ruthless and uncaring. All they want is to put on a good show for the crowds. So I'm telling you right now, you will see some bad things in the months to come. I assure you this."

Buck looked at the two boys. "Do you still want to go for it?"

"Yes. I just hope no one is mistreating my bull because if I catch them, they're toast. That's all I can say." Jacob stared at them.

"Me too! I like your style, Jacob," Tom replied.

"Well, I can give you another thousand right now." He pulled a wad of money out of his pocket and then opened his briefcase and pulled out a contract. The three men looked at Jim as he wrote some words down on a paper and handed it to Jacob. "Sign right here, Jacob, and I'll make it formal later. This makes me your manager."

Jacob looked worried. "My dad always said all an honest man needed was a handshake and an honest face."

"I'll give you that too." He held out his hand. "Son, I'd never betrayed a Bramble. No one in this country would." Jim turned facing Buck, "Am I right, Buck?"

Buck smiled. "No, sir. No one would." Buck looked directly at Tom Rivers. "This is our lucky day, Tom."

Tom smiled and patted his horse on the neck. "Jacob, I do know if he is your manager, he needs your okie dokie to speak for you. And Jim Rogers is well known across the circuit." He stood in silence, then turned to Jacob again. "I've no family to speak of anymore. I'm in all the way, if you'll have me."

Jacob smiled and turned to the men. "Where do I sign?"

Hours later, with the sun straight up over their heads and after having a good lunch, they loaded up the truck and drove off down the highway in the direction of Hatch, New Mexico, like Jim Rogers had asked them to. This was the first rodeo they needed to attend, and they arrived a couple of days before the event was to happen, and this gave Jacob and his new entourage the time required to mend the equipment and oil the saddle before the rodeo was to start. Jacob spent a day making phone calls home, letting the family and Maryann know what he was doing. He made her a promise that he would take good care of himself, that he would someday return home.

The day of the rodeo, he was ready and primed for fun he planned on having. Jim Rogers sat in the stands, watching his new client. Buck and Tom threw the football around with Jacob to get him warmed up. When they called his name on the loudspeaker, Jacob was up and ready to ride.

Buck and Tom prepared the bronco and helped their man climb on its back. And as he was taught, Jacob whispered in its ear some soothing words of respect. Tom watched him closely, and Jacob looked back at him. "No fear." Jacob smiled at him with confidence.

The gate flew open, and the horse took off bucking and jumping high into the air, twisting and jerking but could not throw the rider. Jacob rode him the full eight seconds and jumped off, hearing the loud horn blast off. At the end of the day, Jacob had swept the whole rodeo, finishing first in every event. He was not thrown from any horse or bull and had the fastest time in the steer roping event. He took the winning purse of ten thousand dollars.

Jim Rogers collected the winnings and took his twenty-five percent as his manager and put the rest of the purse to pay for all their food and lodging cost and travel monies for needed expenses. They left Hatch and traveled on to Guthrie, Oklahoma, where Jacob took first again and won more money.

Before leaving, he placed a call home, telling his family about the two rodeos he had participated in. He wasn't concerned about the money, just hoping to catch the trail of Tuff. Jim Rogers continued to book Jacob in several more Oklahoma rodeos, and Jacob kept winning and was having fun. He was at ease with his talents that his dad and grandfather Tuttle had given him in rodeoing. He did his best to inquire about the whereabouts of Tuff, sometimes getting depressed and sad. Buck would encourage him, saying, "Hang in there, kiddo. You're doing just fine."

Months would pass by, and one night, as they were having supper together at a local hotel in Belen, New Mexico, hearing the eating customer's silverware clanging on their plates and the cook yelling out orders up to the waitresses in the restaurant, Jim started outlining their next few days, telling them they were headed to Branson, Missouri. "That's a couple of easy ten-thousand-dollar purses if Jacob keeps sweeping the competition like he has been doing." Smiling, he took a bite of his steak.

The three men sat quietly as they ate, listening to Jim talk. "Then, we can make some big money down in Jacksonville, Florida. Enjoying some competition in the worldwide rodeo association circuit."

"Wait a minute, Jim. I haven't heard you say that you are making inquiries about the whereabouts of Tuff." Jacob frowned.

Buck spoke up, "That's right, Jim! And why are you booking gigs back east?"

Jim Rogers, in his gray two-piece suit and white cowboy hat, looked every bit of his sixty-five years of age, still chewing on his steak, stared at his plate as he talked. "I told you guys, we have to track across the country to build a reputation, and I'm sorry if I neglected to say it may take some serious time. Without a top-notch rep, you're nothing in the rodeo world. Not everybody has heard of the LL Ranch and the Brambles in Tyler, Texas."

Jacob felt sadness at the thought; he thought it would be easier than this. When he played football or baseball at school, he always pulled off the winning runs and throws. In school, he still had the correct equations. When he fell off of a bucking bronco at home, his dad or Ole Cooter always told him how to hold on better next time.

All he wanted was to find his dad's bull, and now he seemed to be getting sidetracked, and he didn't understand why he needed to build a reputation to find Tuff, but holding his peace, and realizing he was young and inexperienced. For some scary moments, he knew his dad wasn't with him anymore, and maybe he needs to listen to this older more experienced rodeo manager.

Still, he was glad Buck and Tom Rivers were here with him. He respected Buck for keeping in touch with his wife, Angie, and also being there for him. He needed both of their support and friendship to help complete his task. In the short months he had been with them, he already felt like they were friends.

Tom Rivers was a quiet young man, and he had told them his story about how he had lost his family in a boating accident a few years back on the Oklahoma Indian reservation, where he had grown up. He was a full-blooded Choctaw Indian and had grown up raising horses and cattle.

The need for making a living had gotten him involved with the prestigious Ty Herder while living in Amarillo, and Tom explained that he allowed specific abuse because the pay was excellent, and he always had food and a roof over his head at night. The dark complexed young man spoke to Jacob, "You know, Jacob, I have seen many broncobusters in my life, but never have I seen someone with the natural talent as you have. You could be one of the best in the world if you wanted."

Jacob smiled and replied, "It must be a gift from God above because I don't care about winning. I just use it hopefully to find Tuff and get him back home."

As the months turned into a year, they had moved on to more significant events in Fort Worth and Del Rio, Texas. They crossed the country traveling to Boise, Idaho, and Vernal, Utah. They competed Las Vegas, and in the Cheyenne, Wyoming, Frontier Days rodeo, and some were saying the "Wonder Kid" from Tyler, Texas, was as good some of the best in the world in the race for the all-around champion.

People were asking in Arlington, Oregon, and the Spokane, Washington, rodeo who he was and where he came from. The interviews started in the North Dakota State Fair and the Denver rodeo. Jacob would telephone his family, but he did not want to go home without Tuff; as much as he wanted to, he just couldn't.

Jim Rogers was relentless in continuing making the deals for Jacob, and he continued to follow the leads, knowing Tuff might forget about him. Jim set a schedule that kept the four men busy and always on the go with the rodeo on their minds; still, Jacob would call home to Tyler, always talking with them on the phone, keeping them updated on what he was doing.

Maryann called Jacob with her cell phone, always keeping him updated on her premed studies at Texas A&M University. Cooter, Sarah, and Luke took care of the LL Ranch with help from the ranch hands who had remained loyal to them. The hands were excited talking about Jacob's travels and hearing on television and in the magazines about his rise to the top of the rodeo circuit and his being called the "Wonder Kid" from Tyler, Texas.

His big sister Jenny was in her last two years of earning her PhD in Special Education specializing in autism in children. She came home often to spend time with the family and the ranch hands that were also considered family.

The LL Ranch was a huge attraction and financial foothold and made a difference in the economy for the city of Tyler. They produced lots of cattle and crops of many types of vegetable, wheat, and corn for the better of the local economy. All the while, their hometown boy Jacob Bramble continued to make the headlines all across the country. A little over two years later and he was still on the hunt for Tuff Bramble who would be four years old now. The Bramble entourage had crossed the country multiple times, staying in motels and once even camped out for a whole week beside the Little Bighorn River in Wyoming.

Only once did Jacob have trouble with other cowboys when he competed in the Cheyenne Frontier Days. He had become enraged watching three cowboys at a time that would wrestle the wild horses down to put a saddle on them to ride around barrels.

And in another competition, they held baby horses that were only weeks old separate from their mothers and release them so the babies would race to find their mothers for money bets. Jacob saw one baby run into the rails and fall, and when it got back up, it was dazed and did not know where it was. Jacob became enraged when the crowd in the stands laughed at what they had seen, and no one went to its aid.

Jacob and Tom ran out on the dirt track to help the baby horse get to its mother, and the owner had tried in vain to stop them. He found himself lying on his belly, coughing up dirt after tangling with the two boys. Jacob had Jim Rogers buy the mother and baby and paid money to send them to live on the LL Ranch in Tyler.

The next week, Jim had gotten them booked in New York City for a national event rodeo at the Madison Square Garden, and after another win, Jacob had taken a cab back to the Waldorf Astoria on Park Avenue. While Buck and Tom were busy taking care of their equipment and collecting the winnings, Jacob went to his room and opened the door the find his mother and brother sitting there, apparently waiting for him to arrive.

Millie stood up and approached him, giving him a much-surprised hug. "Hello, honey! I'm so glad to have finally found you, son. What has it been, two years since we've seen you?"

The now, twenty-year-old Jacob smiled a nervous smile and kissed her on the cheek. "Mother?" His heart told him he was happy to see her.

After the kiss, she replied, "There, that's a better son!" With one of her hands, she caressed Jacobs long blonde hair and the other gently touching his cheek and lips affectionately. "My, my, you've grown some, Jacob. How tall are you now?"

Jacob smiled. "The last physical I had in Montana, the doctor said I was six feet and one inch tall and weighed 185 pounds and healthy," he said.

Willie had stood up and walked over to Jacob. "You're almost as tall as me now, brother." He stood six foot three inches and weighed 210 pounds. He grinned at Jacob with his greased-back hair and blue three-piece custom suit. He stuck out his hand for Jacob to shake hands, and he did. "Hope you don't mind we made ourselves a sandwich from your fridge," Willie remarked, pointing to the coffee table where two plates of food sat almost eaten.

"I don't mind. It's okay," Jacob answered him.

Pushing Willie out of the way, Millie stood in front of Jacob. "Now, son, I'm so glad we have finally gotten to speak with you. We've seen you on television and in the papers doing a perilous and physically demanding job. Have you had any injuries, son?"

Jacob answered, "Some, Mother. I've had a sprained wrist, pulled muscles, bumps, and bruises. It's to be expected for a guy in rodeo. I get up and keep going."

Millie smiled at him. "That's my boy Jacob! Raised on the LL roping and riding, just like his dad."

Quietly, Jacob smiled but did not speak, noticing his brother had walked back over and sat down on the couch and put his feet on the coffee table and started spitting sunflower seeds in the ashtray. "I hear you're pretty good in the rodeo circuit, little bro."

"Of course he's good! He's my son, isn't he?" Millie spoke up, taking her fingers and touching his lips gently. "I'm so proud of you, Jacob, and you've accomplished all this by yourself."

Jacob tried to speak, "Well, not by myself, you see—"

Millie interrupted him, "Well, I hope we'll be seeing a lot more of you, my son." Tenderly, she straightened his shirt collar. "I've missed you so much!"

"I've missed you too, Mom!" he squeezed her hand gently. "But I wanted to tell you—"

Again, she interrupted him, "Honey, your brother and I are here to help guide your career. I want to be your manager!" She smiled. "With my connections in Hollywood and your talent and looks, we'll make it real big, okay?" She made a smile over to Willie, who still sat, spitting out sunflower seeds on the coffee table.

Startled at what she said Jacob spoke up, "Manage my career?"— stepping back suddenly away from her, then catching himself, remembering his dad telling him to be kind to everyone.

"Son?" she replied, looking bewildered.

Jacob walked away from her into the kitchen area and opened the refrigerator and took out a large pitcher of ice tea and poured some into a glass that sat on the counter. Then he sat down on a tall chair stool by the bar and took a long drink before sitting the glass down on the table and began pushing the glass around in circles with his fingers.

His mother came up behind him and began rubbing his shoulders. "What's wrong, honey? I mean, I am your mother."

He stood up and walked over to the sink and put his glass down on it. "It's not that, Mom. It's just that I have a manager. His name is Jim Rogers."

Millie gasped and glanced over at Willie, who had stood up and begun pacing back and forth. She turned to Jacob. "I don't think I know him?"

"No, you don't know him." Jacob was getting red in the face with anger. And not wanting to be rude to his mother, he could not help remembering how both of them had treated his dad.

The anger seemed to explode out of him. "Do you know why I'm in the rodeo circuit?"

"I don't know? Maybe because it comes easy to you, son. You were raised on a ranch." Millie partially grinned.

Jacob frowned and looked at both of them before speaking, "I had to leave home two years ago the day after my high school graduation to go and find me and my dad's Brahma bull. You remember Tuff, don't you? The one that you and Willie sold to the Tyler stockyards on the day my dad was buried." His voice cracked, and his lip quivered; he was so mad at them.

Millie had to think fast, and she continued to try and manipulate him. "Oh, honey, I'm so sorry. I wish you could understand why I did that. Your father was a good man, but naive and simpleminded. He had promised me years earlier that he would take me away from that God-forsaken ranch but never did."

Jacob leaned against the refrigerator and listened to her while his brother paced the living room floor.

"I was fed up with Rory's stubbornness, and I didn't have any money. I had been cheated out of my inheritance. My father only left me a small portion that I sold to your dad before he had died. Rory was a homeless ex-con who was dirty, and he smelled. It was terrible."

Jacob spoke up in an angry voice, "You didn't even have the decency to attend his funeral, and you missed my graduation. How dare you!"

"Listen here, young man. Don't take that tone with me. I'm your mother."

CHAPTER 6

Willie stomped into the kitchen. "Isn't that something, Mom? We came here to help this turd licker, and he treats us like dirt. He's soft like his dad was!"

Jacob gave Willie a hard look. "Don't talk about my father like that, and he was decent and kind. He went to church and took the time to read the Bible every day. He tried to be good to both of you, and you rejected his love," he lashed out.

Millie intervened, "Look here, you sure have a friendly way about the people who raised you, don't you?"

"Raised me? You didn't raise me. My dad and grandfather raised me with the help of Cooter and Sarah and Jenny. You two were never around much, and he"—pointing toward Willie—"and he always picked on me."

"Well, now you sound bitter, Jacob," Millie spoke up. "Don't you even care that we are broke and penniless?"

Jacob blurted out, "You had twenty-five thousand dollars just two years ago, and whatever else you cleared from my dad's account before you left for Hollywood. What happened to it?"

"We lost it all in Las Vegas, and we thought we could double our money. But instead, we lost it all at the crap tables. When we heard about how famous you were becoming, we barely scraped enough to get here. Jacob, the last two years have been hard. Can you understand that, son? I'm your mother. Where will I go? We don't have any money." Millie pleaded for Jacob to feel sorry for them, and he did.

"So here you are trying to be my manager after all this time?" He leaned against the wall and rubbed his face with his hand like he had a headache.

"Well, yes, son. We are family. Remember, blood is thicker than water. Can't you give us some help. We know you are making lots of money right now!"

"Money!" Jacob took a breath. "Is that all you two care about? You haven't even asked about how Cooter and the girls are doing. Did you even know Sarah married Deputy Sheriff Luke Naylor two years ago?"

"I never liked cops!" Willie spoke up.

Jacob started crying at hearing that remark, and he loved Sarah and Luke. He walked away, and they followed him into the bedroom as he pulled open a briefcase that was lying on his bed. He showed them money inside and then closed it and handed it to his mother. "You can take this hundred thousand dollars that I was planning on sending home. You can have it if that's what you want."

"Wow! That's a lot of money. Is this all yours?" Willie gasped.

"I have more than that put away. You can have it, brother. Now I want you both to go away."

Millie smiled in excitement. "Now, about the LL Ranch."

"What about it?" Jacob scorned.

"We are going back to Tyler, and I'm going to get a lawyer to contest Rory's will, then I'll sell it. Now that your father is dead, that place is mine."

Jacob blurted out, "Oh no, it's not! Dad left it to me in his will, and it's up to me who lives there. I don't want you two to ever set foot on the property ever again. Do you hear me?"

"Is that right? I'll sue you for the deed to that ranch, smarty. That place is mine," Millie yelled at him. "My father owned it."

"Go ahead and try. You illegally sold Tuff from the ranch with a forged note that Cooter still has. Luke Naylor and the governor said you ever set foot in Tyler again and they will have both of you arrested, and the deed to the ranch is in mine and Cooter's name. I made sure of that before I left," Jacob embellished a little in his anger.

"You don't frighten me, son. I'm years beyond you."

"Try me, mother. And if you go there, you will go to jail for a long time."

Willie loosened his tie. "Why you punk! I ought to kick your teeth in right now. You think because you're the famous Wonder Kid from Tyler, Texas, that you are somebody? Your nothing to me, and you never were. I was always the better one, and my stepdad Rory knew it."

Although he was not afraid of Willie, Jacob did not want to fight a family member purely out of respect; his dad had taught him to love, not hate. He knew he could not lower himself to their standards.

"Calm down, son," Millie said to Willie. "It's okay. We don't need him or any of the Brambles. Your brother runs with trash now, and he has a fat middle-aged man and a stinking Choctaw Indian with him."

Willie laughed. "Yeah, you're right, mother."

"He's so dumb, he doesn't see that Jim Rogers would sell him out in a minute the first time he can't rodeo anymore." Millie took the briefcase from Willie and turned to walk out, then turned around one more time. "You're a foolish loser just like Rory was. For years, people tried to recruit him for the rodeo circuit, and he refused. I could have taken him to the top, and all he cared about was that damn LL Ranch, and his silly dreams ended up killing him in the end. Look at me. I'm still around." She turned, and Willie followed her out the door and to the elevator.

Jacob felt sick in his stomach. Feeling distraught and homesick for home, he went back to his room, shutting the door behind him, and fell on the bed and cried. Thinking of the mean things his mother had said of his dad made him moan louder. When he finally stopped, he thanked God for Sarah and Jenny and Ole Cooter, whom he loved more than anything in the whole world, and all he wanted to do was go home and be with them.

Meanwhile, Ole Cooter bent over and slowly began to pull the raggedy weeds from around the grave sites at the lower pastures. He had been so busy keeping up with the LL Ranch that he sometimes neglected the plants. Sarah came walking up behind him, still wearing her breakfast apron around her waist. "You miss them, don't you, Cooter?"

Startled by her sudden appearance but mighty pleased to have the company, he answered, "Yes, I do, sweetheart. I never respected any two men in my life as these men. It was good men like them that made our country great."

Sarah smiled. "They loved the LL Ranch a lot, didn't they?" stepping closer and examining the gravesites respectfully.

Cooter took out his handkerchief and wiped the sweat from his eyes. "They wouldn't live anywhere else except this ranch. I remember clearly when Rory first walked off the highway to this place. John told me he could see the love and respect for our ranch in the young man's eyes. He knew what the boy's parents had been through so that they could someday own a ranch of their own. It made Rory want to live here no matter what Millie tried to do to him.

Sarah spoke up, "I remember when Jenny and I first came here, we were frightened at first, coming out of the orphanage to strangers. It didn't take long when you and Daddy Tuttle and Rory made us feel wanted and needed here. Millie never really treated us like family. It was always like we were neighbors or something." She paused. "Sometimes it feels like a bad dream, and I will wake up, they will both be here with us."

Luke Naylor came walking up beside them. "Hi, honey! It's Friday night. Do you want to go out for dinner tonight?" he smiled.

Sarah turned and hugged him. "Sure. Do you want to come with us, Cooter?"

"Oh, that sure sounds wonderful! Are you sure this old codger won't be in your way?"

Luke laughed. "Absolutely, not Cooter. You're more than welcome to come. I'll tell you what? We'll treat you to a big steak tonight."

He turned to Sarah. "Isn't Jenny coming home soon for the summer? The university should have let out by now."

"Well, she called last weekend and asked where Jacob was. I thought she was going to write him a letter. I wonder if she went looking for him."

"Jacob usually calls on Saturday nights to check in, so tomorrow, remember to ask him if he has heard from her."

Cooter excused himself to get cleaned up for supper.

Several hours later, they were on the twenty-minute drive into Tyler in Luke's Econovan. Sarah rode up front in the passenger seat, and Cooter rode in the back seat. He enjoyed watching the young couple laugh and talk together and thought about how nice they fit together.

They had been such a big help with Jacob and Rory gone, and Luke had referred three of the new hands from his contacts as a deputy and knowing other ranchers in the county around them. Still, Cooter felt like crying every time he thought about Rory and young Jacob. The newspapers wrote about the "Wonder Kid" from Tyler that could not be thrown; his father would be so proud of him.

While Cooter cried in Tyler, Jacob was at that very moment crying in New York City. He had his face buried in his pillow and sobbed uncontrollably for a few minutes. "Why, God? Why does my mother have to be that way, so hateful and bitter against my dad? Why did you have to take my dad from me? Why is it taking so long to find Tuff? I understand that faith is something unseen that we have to believe in, but it's so hard to keep having faith. What will I do if I never find him? Oh, my goodness! I can't think like that," he cried.

Jacob was distraught and lonely in his heart for his family back home; he cried for them and even harder when he thought about the horrible things his mother and Willie said about his dad. Rory Bramble had been a good father and never once failing his son. He was a proud dad who had nurtured and mentored him to manhood, never turning his back on him.

He thanked God for Ole Cooter and Sarah and Jenny. Then he was thankful Sarah had married Luke, a proper law officer. Feeling distraught, Jacob went into the bathroom and washed his face and brushed his teeth, then he walked through the living room area of the room and grabbed up his cowboy hat and left going to the elevator and went down to the lobby.

He looked around at the people coming and going in the lobby and wondered what to do; he just needed to get some fresh air and think for a while. He walked out of the hotel and gave the hotel front door valet fifty dollars. "I'm Jacob Bramble."

The man answered, "I know who you are, sir!"

Jacob smiled a nervous smile. "When my friends arrive from the Madison Square Garden, can you tell them I'll be back in a couple of hours? I just need to go for a walk." And he walked away down the street.

He walked up Park Avenue for a while, just thinking. The thoughts of how much he missed his family back home were so surreal, and he was getting stares from people passing him, seeing a cowboy wearing a cowboy hat walking the downtown streets of New York City.

An hour later, he came to a towering church Steeple and stopped and stared a moment, then decided to go inside. Although he was not of the Catholic faith, for some reason, he didn't care right now. He walked inside the building and saw a large room with many pews and seats to sit on, and there were several people kneeling on the knees in the positions that appear to be praying.

The room was large and spacious with a pulpit at the front and many large colorful windows with varied colors. He removed his hat and went and sat about halfway up the aisle, thinking this was nothing like the Assemblies of God churches he had grown up in. Still, he somehow felt at ease and comforted by the large portraits of Jesus cupping his hands as if he were praying. He sat down in a seat and got down on his knees and started praying, but the right words would not come to him, but he still chanted on, and the confusion that ached his heart overcame his desire to pray.

He sat up and then sat back in his seat and just watched the people come and go. He was amazed at how quiet they were. Seeing some of the people going inside small rooms on the side of the seating area, he watched for a while, then he stood up and walked over to one, watching an older lady come out of one.

Figuring out that it was a confession booth, he opened the wooden door and went inside and sat down. A small window opened from the other side, and a priest he assumed said some holy words and then asked what he would like to confess to.

Jacob spoke up, "Father, I'm not of the Catholic faith, sir."

The priest answered back, "That won't be held against you, son. What would you like to confess to me?"

He replied, "My heart aches to be clean of my sins. I have disrespected my mother, and I have some bad feelings for her and my brother."

"Has something happened to cause these feelings, my son?"

Jacob answered him, "Yes, father. It's been two years since my father passed away, and I still have bad feelings for the way my mother and my brother behaved during this time. I have carried bad feelings in my heart for that time, and today I told both of them what they did."

The priest said, "Sometimes things happen in life that tend to drag us down. We want everything to be perfect and blissful. That isn't the way life works, and we live in an imperfect world that can be challenging for us. We have to work at finding peace."

"I know that, sir, but they took something from me that represented the bond I had with my father, and I can't seem to be able to forgive them."

The priest spoke again, "Son, Jesus said no one is without sin. We are born into it and fight with it all the days of our life. I think you need to find something that brings you to the joy you remembered at home and do it. Forgive those that trespass against you, and you will find peace."

Jacob thought of the words the priest had told him and said, "Yes, thank you, sir! I will make every effort to remember your words."

"Read your Bible and follow the life of Jesus, son."

Jacob thanked him and left, stopping by the front door, and he left five hundred dollars in the church offering box. He turned around once more and said, "Thank you, God, for your help!" Then it came to him to go to a local hospital and visit the patients.

He walked six or seven blocks and came to a hospital with a sign that said Mount Sinai Hospital, and he went inside. Looking around, he approached an information desk and spoke to an elderly lady, "Ma'am, I've some experience with someone who had cancer, and I'd like to volunteer to spend some time with some of your patients."

The lady looked at him. "That's a wonderful offer, young man. Let me get a supervisor of the oncology department to come to talk with you."

As he waited standing there, some of the kids being pushed around in a wheelchair saw him waiting and approached him. "Aren't you Jacob Bramble, the Wonder Kid from Tyler, Texas."

Jacob removed his hat and smiled at the girl of about twelve years old. "Why, yes, I am."

The girl smiled, seemingly to cheer up. "My brothers just went to the Madison Square Garden and saw you this morning."

Jacob was pleased. "Yes, I was there. How are you doing, sweetheart?"

"I'm okay, considering," she answered him as her orderly realized Jacob was a famous rodeo man.

People started gathering around to see him as the supervisor came to talk with him. "So, you are Jacob Bramble?" the supervisor asked.

"Yes, ma'am, I am. The reason I'm here is that when I was fourteen, my best friend went through a battle with cancer, and she beat it. I remember the ups and downs of the whole process, and since I was here in New York for the day, I'd like to help out if I could."

She smiled at him. "Well, we could go up to the second floor to the recovering patients' unit, and you could talk with some of our younger patients if you want to."

Jacob answered, "I'd love to, ma'am!"

She walked him to the elevator, and they went to the second floor, and he was amazed to see so many patients and some in their wheelchairs. Right away, he started talking with them and trying to bring their spirits up. Some of the parents began taking pictures and asking for autographs that he gladly gave, and he went out of his way to get the photos with the kids and him together.

He stood in the middle of the room so he could address all the children and talked with them as they asked him questions about roping and riding horses and about the bucking bulls that looked real scary on television. Then he started going to each bed and tried to talk with the sicker and weaker patients. He held their hands and kissed them on the foreheads and tucked in their bedsheets for them.

He had been there for hours, and he knew he must get back to the hotel, so he attempted to say goodbye to them. He saw one boy about eight years old lying in his bed quiet and reserved, so he walked over to the boy and pulled up a chair beside him and sat down. "Hello there, young man!"

"Hi!" the boy answered him with his dad standing nearby.

Jacob could see the boy was weak and looked tired; he tried to be helpful and positive for the boy. "How are you doing today, young man?" approaching the boy's hospital bed in a friendly manner.

He was weak and could barely speak. "I'm good, Jacob."

"So you know my name?"

The boy smiled at him. "I have heard everyone talking with you."

Jacob reached down and gently picked up his hand. "What's your name?"

He answered, "I'm Ethan Grant III." He squinted from pain, and Jacob could feel his little hand quivering.

"Well, Ethan Grant III, I'm delighted to meet you!" Looking at his father, he asked, "Is this Dad?"

Ethan managed a smile. "Yes, he's the best dad in the whole..." to exhausted to finish. His father looked like he wanted to cry but stood his ground.

"I'm sure he is Ethan. Well, son"—he stroked his hand gently—"would you like to ask me anything today?"

The little boy grunted a little in pain. "Yes, I would, Jacob."

Jacob smiled. "Good, Ethan. What can I help you with?" he asked, looking at the intravenous pain medication dripping and giving the boy large doses to ease his pain.

Ethan took a breath and said, "Can you help my dad? My mother died three years ago, and I'm afraid I will be going to heaven soon to be with her, and he will be alone. My dad has been through so much. I worry for him."

Jacob just about started crying. "Yes, little man, and I'll personally make sure your dad is taken care of. But Ethan, you're going to be okay, I promise. Just remember your dad and your mother and Jesus are with you always."

"Thank you, Jacob, and will you remember me when you win the championship I hear you will be going to? I heard my friends here talking about you."

"You bet I will, Ethan. Now, I want you to get some rest so you'll get better, okay?"

"Yes, Jacob, I will. You made me a promise, and I can make you a promise." And he closed his eyes and went to sleep because of the medicine he was taking. The nurse checked on him and looked at Jacob and winked.

"Is he okay?"

"Yes, he's just sleeping. That's all. Ethan is a good boy!" she said to him.

Jacob stood up and turned to his father. "Here, Ethan II, this is my sister's phone number. I want you to call her. Her name is Sarah. She will give you a job and a place to live anytime you need, okay?"

"I can't leave my son," he answered.

Jacob pulled out the rest of the money in his pocket and handed him five thousand dollars in cash. "Of course you can't, sir. This is for both of you, and if you ever need to call my sister, I'll tell her to take care of you. Do you understand?"

He looked at Jacob and took the money and put it in his pocket. "Yes, I do. Thank you, Jacob."

Jacob had left the hospital, and as he walked back toward the hotel, he called Sarah on his cell phone, and he told her about his day and Ethan and his father. She complied and pledged to do whatever she could if he called her.

An hour late, he had returned to the hotel room, and he felt refreshed and happy that he had done something right. That priest had given him some good advice. His three friends had been waiting for him; the hotel valet had given them his message. Jacob told them what he had been doing, about Ethan and his father, and what his mother and brother had done.

"I'm sorry to hear this, Jacob, although I do have some good news for you," Jim Rogers spoke up.

Jacob perked up a bit. "What, Jim? I could use some good news about now."

"Well, it seems through my sources, I have contacted a man who thinks he may know about Tuff."

Smiling, Jacob said, "That's great! All right," giving Tom and Buck a high five hand slap.

"There is a man who lives in Fort Wayne, Indiana, and his name is Steve Purdue," Rogers explained.

"Is Tuff in Indiana, Jim?" Tom asked.

"No, but we are going to compete in the Huntingdon rodeo that is near Fort Wayne. Steve is my contact to get us in, and he also has a daughter who barrel races in that rodeo event. I told him about our quest, and he said he heard about Jacob," Jim replied.

Buck smiled. "What has he heard, Jim?" Settling down in a leather recliner and sipping on his cup of hot coffee.

"Steve said he has contacts all over the country in the rodeo circuit and has heard the talk of all the ones we have been to asking questions about this Brahma bull."

"Oh yeah?" Buck inquired.

"Well, Steve said there is a Brahma named Tornado that is black with white markings on his face like Tuff. He was the meanest bull on the West Coast. Cowboys fear him, and he thinks his dad just bought him."

CHAPTER 7

Jacob was happy and began dancing around the room with Tom whooping and hollering! Now he knew that he was getting close to finding his Brahma, and he could go home soon back to Tyler. "Let's go get him, Jim."

Jim took a breath and grinned. "We will see soon, after we get the facts straight and after the Huntingdon rodeo. Don't get so pumped up yet, and we don't know if it's true. We'll have to go to Fort Wayne first." He took a puff on his cigar. "And the purse in Huntingdon is a cool thirty thousand dollars."

The four men calmed down and thought for a second. "All right then, whatever it takes!" Jacob smiled.

That evening went by quickly, and the next morning, they had loaded up the trucks and pulled out of New York. Buck drove his truck, pulling behind their trailer and gear, and Jacob and Tom followed behind them, Jim had taken a taxi to the airport.

Tom stared out the passenger window at the big city they were leaving behind. "There sure are a lot of people in New York, huh, Jacob?"

With his hands gripping the truck's steering wheel, Jacob looked at him and smiled. "Yes. I don't think I would want to live here. That's for sure. Give me the open plains and prairie dogs peeking up from their holes in the ground."

"Yeah, me too!" Tom added. "I miss my home in Oklahoma. I always had family around me, and I was happy back then. We rode horses and fished and spent many happy times together. Now, I have no one, and sometimes when I think about it, it scares me to be alone in this world."

Jacob could feel the loneliness in his voice, trying to drive and follow Buck yet listening to Tom talk. "God knows all the answers, Tom, and someday when we get up there, maybe he'll enlighten us on those secrets."

Tom looked at Jacob and smiled. "Yes, I think so too, Jacob."

"Tom, when this is all over, I want you and Buck and Angie to come live in Tyler on the LL Ranch with my family and me. They will love you and take care of you. I promise you that!"

Tears filled Tom's eyes. "Buck has Angie to think of, but I will think about it, Jacob." He wiped his eyes. "Thank you!" Staring out the window, he said, "Jacob, answer me one thing, though?"

"Anything, buddy." Jacob grinned.

"Well, for two years now, you have referred to your ranch as the LL. What does the LL mean?" Tom smiled.

"It's not commonly told, but my grandfather John Tuttle said he named it after his wife, my grandmother I never knew because she died even before my dad came to Tyler. He named it the Lucky Lady Ranch."

Tom smiled, looking out the window. "The Lucky Lady? Hmm. Makes sense, Jacob. I like it! Thank you for sharing that!"

"Sure." Jacob kept driving.

More than a day later, they arrived in Fort Wayne and drove to Steve's house. Pulling up in front of the house, they climbed out of their trucks, and Jim Rogers came walking out the front door with Steve.

Buck yelled toward Jim, "I take it your flight was good?"

"Yes, I have a hotel room by the airport, and Steve came and picked me up. We already have the entries signed up for Huntingdon tomorrow, and Steve's wife has graciously cooked us dinner. It'll be ready in a few minutes."

"Perfect! We brought our feed bags with us!" Buck laughed.

Steve stepped forward and shook hands with Buck and Tom, then looked at Jacob. "So this is the Wonder Kid from Tyler, Texas?"

Jacob shook his hand. "Well, I don't know about that, sir. That's just a title that I picked up along the way." Smiling, he shook hands with Steve and then his wife, Pam, who came out the front door wearing her apron around her waist.

Steve laughed. "I'll say, in the last two years, you have made an impact on the pro rodeo circuit. You came out of nowhere and rocked the cowboys all across the country. I'm honored to have you guys stay the night in our home."

"I want no fuss, sir. I'm on a mission. That's all. Then I want to go back home."

Steve grinned. "That's what your manager, Jim, has told us. But it's hard to digest reading the pro rodeo magazines and watching you on television for the last two years, so humble and honest in today's world." Steve laughed. "God bless America!"

"Yes, sir!" Jacob smiled.

"I sure would have liked to meet the parents who raised you, son. They did one heck of a job!"

Jacob answered, "I would have given all of this away to see my grandparents Campbell and Ellie Bramble and John Tuttle and my father, Rory Bramble, to be alive today and with me. Then I could have just gone on the college with my best girl Maryann."

Steve hugged Pam and spoke up, "That's says everything about you right there, Jacob, and we appreciate your story."

They all went inside the house and sat down to a nice dinner and later talked about drinking coffee in the living room. Steve told them about his parents in Tucson who might have some informa-tion about Tornado or Tuff. Steve gave them his parents' information in Tucson and wished them well. They planned to compete in the Huntingdon rodeo and then head to Arizona to find Steve's family, and hopefully soon, they would have Tuff and go back home.

The next morning, they drove down the thirty miles to Huntington, Indiana. Hours later, Jacob was preparing to ride; the bronco he had drawn was jumping around in the stall. "Hold him steady, Tom, so I can climb down on him." Lowering himself down, he whispered his secret message into the bronco's ear.

Jacob wrapped the leather strap around his left hand that was holding the saddle horn and winked at Tom. The gate swung open, and off they went. The horse jumped and twisted and kicked high in the air but could not throw Jacob off of his back. The eight-second buzzer sounded off, and Jacob loosened the leather strap and jumped off and landed in the dirt arena on his feet and ran to the rails and climbed up and over the stall.

Jacob watched Steve's daughter Leslie barrel race and gave her some helpful tips, and with Buck and Tom's help, he went on to lead the scoring and again picked up the thirty-thousand-dollar purse. Jacob insisted on Jim giving half of it to Steve and Leslie for their courtesy of feeding and putting up his entourage and keeping their whereabouts a secret. Mostly, everywhere they went, the reporters and photographers would follow them.

The next morning after breakfast with Steve and his family, the entourage left, driving toward Arizona and the Purdue Ranch in Tucson. Jacob could hardly wait; he was getting closer to finding Tuff than ever before.

After three days of driving, in the evening time, they had arrived in Tucson. Driving toward the Purdue Ranch off of Marsh Station Road, with the light of the moon shining down, Buck had noticed a truck that was stuck down in the sandy wash as they drove over the Cienega Bridge. It was a way up the washes and appeared to be dug in deep like it had crashed into a pile of dirt. Not giving it much thought, they traveled on.

Continuing, they came to an overhead sign that read Purdue Ranch, they turned into the driveway and followed it to the main house. When their headlights hit the houses, automatic security sensor lights came on, giving them a bright, clear view of the front door. The front door opened, and a big man came outside, and the three men parked their trucks and walked up to the door. "We're sorry to arrive so late, sir. Are you, Mr. Purdue?" Buck asked, reaching out his hand to shake.

"Yes, I am. Glad to meet you, boys. My son Steve told me you were coming in." He shook all of their hands. "I'm afraid we have a big problem right now, and I can't reach my other sons."

"Well, maybe we can help, Mr. Purdue," Tom offered. "What do you need?"

"Well, the Brahma I purchased and Jacob's sister Jenny have disappeared. I could not find them, so I called the Pima County Sheriff's Office, and they supposedly have a search going on right now. I haven't heard from anyone."

Jacob burst out, "What's my sister doing here?"

Seeing Jacob was alarmed, Mr. Purdue said, "She came here a couple of days ago to look at Tornado. She planned on staying on till you arrived. My wife and I had to go to Marana for a while, and when we got home this morning, she and the bull were gone, and so is my brown work truck."

Buck thought for a second then spoke up, "Did you say a brown truck?"

"Yes, Buck, why?" Jim answered.

"On the way here, I could see by the light of the full moon a brown truck in the wash below. It looked as if someone had some trouble."

Tom spoke up, "I could track her, Jacob."

Jim Purdue spoke up, "You'll need some of my best horses to get through that deep wash. Go to the barn and saddle up, take what you need boys!"

Tom and Jacob ran to the barn and saddled up two good horses. In their saddles carrying a rope with them, the two men followed Buck and Jim in Jacob's truck. They went back to the bridge, and Jim quickly confirmed it was his truck. They could not find Jenny. Buck and Jim stayed up on the ridge alongside the wash and drove slowly with the truck's headlights on while Tom and Jacob rode their horses through the sandy wash looking for Jenny. With only the moonlight to help them see, they had traveled three miles or more slowly when Tom saw something up ahead of them. There looked to be some coyotes barking and surrounding something lying in the sand. "Jacob!" he yelled, pointing up forward.

Their horses took off in a fast lope toward the coyotes, and the two men twirled their ropes round and round, yelling and screaming to frighten off the coyotes. Buck followed them up on the ledge above with his headlights on. When they arrived, they found a body lying in the sand, not moving, and the coyotes ran off in fear of the noise.

"Jenny!" Jacob yelled out, seeing her lying in the sand. He dropped his rope and jumped off of the horse and ran to her with Tom right beside him.

She opened her eyes slowly; she was fragile. "Jacob, you found me."

He reached down and touched her face." Yes, Jenny, I'm here. We'll get you out of here. You're okay now. I got you, sis!" He picked her up and ran her up the side of the wash and put her in the truck and jumped in beside her in the back seat."

Tom retrieved Jacob's horse, and they climbed the side of the wash. "Don't worry about me, guys. Get her to a hospital, and I'll take the horses back to the barn."

Jim pointed Buck in the direction of the hospital, and they made their way to the freeway and on toward town. It took about twenty-five minutes, and they arrived at the Tucson Medical Center emergency room. Jacob picked her up and carried her inside to the emergency room.

It was about three o'clock in the morning when the doctors felt she was well and settled enough to be moved to her room. She had suffered dehydration and hunger but was going to pull through. Jacob insisted on staying with her while Jim and Buck went back to the Purdue Ranch.

Around eight o'clock, the hospital food trays were being distributed to the patients in their rooms. One of the nurses recognized the Wonder Kid and got him a food tray to eat with his sister in her room. As they ate breakfast together, Jenny was feeling better, and they talked. "Oh, Jacob, I'm so glad you found me!"

He smiled as he ate. "Me too!"

"How did you find me, brother?" she asked while she ate a piece of toast.

"I guess it was good timing. My manager, Jim Rogers, had sent us to Tucson to the Purdue Ranch, and when we got there, Mr. Purdue told us you had disappeared with his brown truck. My friend

Buck luckily had seen a truck stuck in the wash from the bridge we crossed, and we went there to look for you."

"I thought I was a goner, Jacob." Tears filled her eyes.

"Well, you're just fine now, sister. I called home, and Sarah and Luke are on their way here to get you. They said you didn't call them when you got out of school for the summer. They've been worried sick for you, Jenny."

She looked at him with sympathetic eyes. "I wanted to see my little brother. We haven't seen you in over two years now, Jacob. Before I left school for the summer, I searched on the Internet for recent sales of Brahmas and found the Purdue's had recently purchased one, so I went to see them. I wanted to help you, Jacob, so you would come back home."

He stood up and carried his empty tray and sat it on the counter next to her bed and drank up his cup of tea. "Don't worry, Jen. I am coming home soon. That's all I want…believe me, sister. I love my family more than anything in the world." He reached out and hugged her and kissed her on the forehead gently.

"Really?" She looked at him.

"Of course, really!" He smiled and sat back down.

She smiled at him and spoke up, "Jacob, you've grown some, and you're a very handsome young man, but you need a haircut." She laughed.

"I guess I do at that." He laughed with her.

Jenny cautiously positioned herself with her elbows and sat up in bed, "I think we are on the right trail, brother."

"You do? Why?"

"Well, the Purdues did have Tuff."

"Well, I was told they had a Brahma named Tornado that they had bought from a dealer out in California," Jacob told her.

"Yes, but it's Tuff, Jacob. I swear to God. I saw him, and I know Tuff."

"Is he still there?" Jacob looked excited.

"I went into their barn, and I saw him, and he recognized me. He has the white star on his face, and he had grown, Jacob. Like you, he's bigger but was gentle with me."

"What happened, Jenny? How did you end up in that wash at Cienega Creek?"

"Well, I was talking with Tuff when four men came in the barn and said they were taking him. They told me Millie had paid them to steal him and take him to Sedona, Arizona, for the national championship rodeo."

"What? Was Mother and Willie with them?" Jacob began getting angry.

"No, the men said Millie Bramble was going to sell him in Sedona and split the sixty thousand dollars with them. She told them Ty Herder, the contender for the championship title, was going to buy him."

"I saw her and Willie in New York after the Madison Square Garden event and paid her one hundred thousand dollars to go away."

"You did?" she answered him.

"Yes. I thought that would be the end of her for good. She complained about losing the LL Ranch to Dad."

"I told those men that Tuff belonged to you and my adoptive father, Rory, and the story of your chase for him, and they said everyone had heard that silly story. But Ty Herder wants Tuff for some vendetta against you."

Jacob frowned and thought for a second before speaking. He stood up and walked to the window and looked outside in the garden area. "When I first started looking for Tuff, my first stop was in Amarillo. Ty was practicing riding broncos, and I guess I laughed at him. After I showed him up, he left, but Bucks wife, Angie, who runs the restaurant there, told me he was asking questions about me before he left. I think she told him I was looking for Tuff."

"You've become famous since then, Jacob, and all of America knows what you want. I guess secrets are hard to keep."

"Yes, I've found out that there is a price to pay for fame. Everyone knows your business." He ran his hands through his long brown hair.

"Well, those men told me they were taking me with them, so I ran away and found the keys in that truck and drove away. They chased me as far as the wash, and I guess they figured I crashed the truck, so they left."

"Yes, and Jim Purdue said his Brahma was gone, so they took him."

"What are you going to do now, little brother? How will you find him now?"

"I'm not going to leave here till Sarah and Luke get here. Mr. Purdue has extended his home for us as long as we need, he said. So maybe we'll stay at the Purdues' for some time till my manager can get us booked into the Sedona rodeo." He smiled and bent over and kissed her on the cheek, then sat back down in the chair and waited.

Five days later, they had spent some quality time at the Purdues' resting and enjoying the warm Tucson weather. Jim Rogers had booked them in the Sedona championship rodeo, and they were making preparations. Sarah and Luke had taken Jenny out of the TMC Hospital and returned her to the Purdue Ranch. Jim and Georgia Purdue just loved having everyone there with them.

Luke Naylor had addressed the kidnap attempt and theft of Tuff to the Pima County Sheriff's Department, with his credentials being a sheriff in Tyler. He knew the extravagance and the laws, assuring Pima County he would make every attempt to keep them informed of any changes.

Sarah and Jenny were thrilled to be able to spend time with Jacob and his new friends. Jacob informed them that Buck and Tom would be returning to live at the LL Ranch when this was all over, and they loved the idea. Both men had earned home and proved their loyalty after all they had been through with Jacob.

It was a nice, relaxing break for everyone, knowing where Tuff was headed, and now they could focus on the last leg of the trip, and they enjoyed the hospitality of the Purdues. But now, everyone wanted to complete the journey, and everyone was going to Sedona, even the Purdues.

At that very moment, Millie and Willie were in Sedona in a restaurant meeting with Ty Herder. Between bites of his Porterhouse steak, Ty spoke up, "Millie, I've already paid you the sixty thousand for that black Brahma. I have him in Will Gibson's stockyard housed in a stall over there in the rodeo grounds' barn. Now I want to win that championship title, and your son Jacob could take it from me."

Millie smiled. "He's good, Ty. Outstanding! The ratings are all in his favor."

Ty screamed at her, "I know that, lady! That's where you come in. His manager has already registered him, but no one knows where he is. I want you to find him and stop him at any cost, and if you do, I'll give you half of that 250 thousand dollars first prize money."

Millie smiled at Willie, who seemed to be not paying attention as he ate. She spoke up, "That's a lot of money, Ty."

"Yes, I know, lady. I'll make that up easily with endorsements and special personal appearances for the next year. That boy of yours is good, and the polls have him in the lead. So far, he has never been beaten. If I were the one to bring down the Wonder Kid, I'd be more famous than I am."

Three days later, Jacob and his entourage had left Tucson and drove north to Sedona, Arizona. The traffic was terrible as the rodeo was a massive event in Sedona. There were to be fifteen of the best cowboys from all over the country that was fierce competitors wanting to win some of the biggest prizes in the country. This was a special event, with cowboys attempting to get the championship title of the world.

Jacob cautiously drove his truck behind Buck, seemingly unnoticed at this point, and he was smiling from ear to ear, mostly eager to see Tuff again. Jim Rogers had told them the Sedona stockyard manager, Will Gibson, confirmed Tuff was here being kept in the barn by the arena.

His loyal worker Chaco had been caring for him. Luke Naylor followed behind Jacob in his car, driving Sarah and Jenny and the Purdues. They smiled and gazed out of the windows at the large crowds. Sarah pointed out the national and local news crews were everywhere. The entourage made it to the arena where a large banner hung overhead read, "Sedona's Professional Rodeo Cowboys Association 2014 World Championship."

Tom looked at Jacob. "You will be competing against only the best cowboys from all over the country, Jacob. Are you nervous?"

Jacob grinned. "About the rodeo? No. When I think about seeing Tuff again, yes. This is what I have worked for. I'm tired of this rodeo stuff, Tom, and I want to get Tuff and go back home for good."

Buck was waved down by two men, and he came to a stop. Jacob watched him talking, and then they waived everyone on by, and Tom rolled down his window, passing the two men. "Jim, glad to see ya!"

Jim Rogers smiled, pointing to the man next to him. "The rodeo has been going on for days now with the lower-ranking cowboys getting their shots first, boys. Jacob is to start tomorrow. This is Will Gibson, and this is our final destination, boys. Tuff is over there in the barn."

Jacob let out a scream in excitement! "Let's get parked and go see him."

They parked their vehicles, and everyone got out and stood as Jim Rogers and Will approached them. Will yelled and waved his assistant to them. "This is Chaco, my main worker and assistant here in Sedona."

Buck reached out his hand and shook Chaco's. "Chaco, glad to meet you, son"—looking at the sixteen-year-old Indian boy.

"Nice to meet all of you!" he answered.

Will spoke up, "This young man is the son of my good friend Chief Big Eagle. His father and I served in World War II together. Big Eagle is the chief of the Navajo Indians. They live on the Navajo reservation about ten miles north of here. He's a big help to me. With all the care needed for the rodeo stock here, he's a real top hand!"

CHAPTER 8

Jacob and the others stared at the boy's blackened eye. "My brother Willie did this?" Jacob asked, taking his finger gently and touched Chaco's swollen eye.

"Yes," Chaco replied.

"I'm sorry, young man," Jacob said, looking back at Sarah and Jenny.

Chaco suddenly perked up. "Are you the real Jacob Bramble, the Wonder Kid from Tyler, Texas?"—his face grinning from ear to ear.

"Yes, I am, Chaco. I want to thank you for taking care of Tuff. I have been searching for him for over two years now!"

Chaco smiled and removed his cowboy hat and held it out for Jacob. "Will you sign my hat, sir?"

Jacob quietly laughed. "Of course I will. I'd be happy to, son!"

"Mr. Bramble, when my boss told me what your manager had told him about this story, I was honored to be Tuff's friend. He's a good bull, very friendly, and I see so much good in him, even though he has a bad reputation for being mean."

"Thank you, son, and call me Jacob, like my friends do."

Chaco looked at Tom, "Sir, are you Navajo?"—looking at the handsome six-foot-tall Indian wearing a Stetson cowboy hat.

He smiled, patting Chaco on the shoulder gently. "No, son, I am Choctaw of the Chippewa and Choctaw Indians of the Oklahoma reservation. I work for Jacob Bramble." Then he took his hand and gently touched Chaco's bruised face.

Chaco held out his hat again. "Will you sign my hat too? I read about you in the Rodeo Events magazine. They say that without your help, the Wonder Kid would not be where he was!"

Tom smiled. "Why thank you, Chaco. I'd be honored to sign your hat!"

Chaco was so excited to be talking to Jacob and Tom, he almost forgot to extend his father's invitation for this evening. "By the way, my father wanted me to ask all of you to come to stay the night with us as our guest."

Jim Rogers was taken by surprise at the invitation but quickly realized it would be a great way to hide from the media; if anyone were on the lookout for Jacob, the last place they would think to look would be on the Navajo reservation. "We would be honored to accept your father's invitation, Chaco."

Will walked over to Jim Purdue. "Jim, I understand Tuff was stolen from your ranch in Tucson?"

"Yes, sir, he was." Jim and Georgia stood together next to Sarah, Jenny, and Luke.

"Well, Millie Bramble claims he is hers, and she had four cowboys bring him here a week or so ago for the rodeo. I say we don't let on we know the truth just yet."

"Is Millie and Willie around here today?" Jenny spoke up. "I have got a few words to say to her if I could."

"I haven't seen them today, but their hired cowboys are watching the barn where Tuff is being kept. They have tried to starve him and keep him from water to weaken him for Ty Herder, but that bull is strong. Ty is afraid of him. Chaco tried to get him water, and that's when Willie caught him."

Luke stepped up. "Will, I'm a deputy sheriff from Tyler. I'm also Jacob's brother-in-law. Have you called the local sheriffs about this?"

"No, Luke. I'm just the proprietor here. I rent stalls and charge for feeding the animals. Millie paid me to keep him in the barn just till after the rodeo. I think she plans on selling him. I only learned that Tuff was stolen from Jim Rogers. But Mr. and Mrs. Purdue as the rightful owners could report the theft."

Georgia Purdue spoke up, "No, we don't want to do that, Will. We have already given him back to the Brambles. He belonged to Rory and Jacob. He was their baby that they raised together, and we don't want him back."

Will looked at them. "That's very thoughtful of you two."

"Well, that's the right thing to do." Jim Purdue smiled.

"Well, okay then! Everybody follow me," Will chirped. He led them through a side entrance into the barn, hoping not to be noticed by Millie's hired cowboys. They stopped by a stall that held a big black Brahma bull, and everyone turned to watch Jacob's reaction. He got closer to the booth and stood there, looking the animal over as he got choked up with feelings.

"Be careful, Jacob." Sarah pulled back on his shirt. "It might not be him."

Jacob ignored her and climbed into the stall with the bull. Looking for marks he knew Tuff had, he checked behind his right ear for a lump, then the white star on his forehead. Then he looked at his hoofs—three black ones and his left back foot were white.

Jacob picked with a wire brush and began brushing back the black fur by his left rear leg and exposed a small letter J that had been branded into him as a baby. "Oh, my Tuff!" Jacob wept as the others watched him. "I cried when Dad branded him, thinking it hurt him. And now I know my dad was smart in doing this. This is Tuff!"

The Brahma seemed to respond to Jacob; he didn't move too much, and he let Jacob hug him. With Jacob's arm around his neck, the bull licked him and mooed with grateful relief; he had been reunited with his best friend after more than two years.

Jim Purdue spoke up, "That's his bull, all right. So the California Tornado is Tuff Bramble!"

"Oh, Tuff, I've missed you, baby! Don't worry. I'm going to get you back home. I promise!" Jacob wept.

As they stood around in the happy moment, they did not know that Millie had cracked open the barn door just enough to hear the conversations. Looking inside, she was surprised to see Will Gibson talking with Jim Rogers, the legendary manager of Jacob Bramble.

She was startled to see Sarah and Jenny with them. She was furious at Will Gibson for the trick he was trying to play on her, she thought; she realized she must be cautious now. Quietly, she would sneak away to warn Willie. She frantically fought her way through the ever-increasing crowds of people.

Knowing Jacob and his friends did not want to be seen by the press, she headed straight for a crewman of one of the news stations. "Hey, how much would you give me to tell you where Jacob Bramble is right now?"

The man had long grungy-looking hair and appeared to be around the age of thirty. He stopped and looked at Millie. "How do you know where he is? We haven't seen him drive in yet."

Millie slanted him a stare with sullen eyes. "Mister, I don't give anything away for free. I asked you what is worth to you."

He glared a distrusting look at her, then handed her a hundred dollars. "Will this work?" he asked.

"The Wonder Kid they call him is over there"—se pointed—"in that barn looking at a bull."

Overhearing Millie's conversation, Chaco's sisters dashed to the barn and bolted through the front door. "Quick, Chaco. That woman Millie knows you're here, and she just told a news cameraman," they yelled.

Everyone ran out the side door and went to Will's office by the arena and went inside and shut the door. The newsman arrived in the barn, and no one was there. "Dang it! I just got ripped off." And he went back to where he was with a sigh of disgust.

Millie had found Willie next to the concession stand, eating a hotdog and drinking a soda. "Let's go, Willie! Jacob and his entourage are here now, and they've found Tuff."

He followed her to the cowboys that were sitting at a picnic table, drinking beer and laughing it up. "Okay, cowboys, I'm paying you good money to stay sober and keep your wits about you," she yelled at them with her hands on her hips.

"Aw, come on, Millie! It's party time," one of them coaxed her.

"You can party on your time, mister. Right now, I need you four to follow Jacob around the arena, and don't let him out of your sight."

They seemed to sober up after hearing his name, and they had only seen him on television and in the newspapers, but they realized he was someone to reckon with in the rodeo ring. "Where is he? Did you see him?" one of them asked.

She pointed toward the barn. "He was just over there in the barn with that bull, and he's not alone. Be careful not to be seen stalking him." She seemed nervous and angry.

By the time they arrived at the barn, Jacob's entourage had already left for the Navajo reservation; they were too late. But knowing he was in Sedona, they figured to wait him out; they could still stop him from competing in the rodeo.

But at that very moment, Jacob sat looking out the truck window. He let Tom do the driving as they followed the two trucks in front of them toward the Navajo Indian reservation. "Isn't this beautiful country, Tom?"—letting the fresh air blow his long wavy hair with the window rolled down.

"It sure is, Jacob. It's so vast, and the mountain air is incredible. Everywhere you look, there are trees so full of colorful leaves. This Arizona high country is so much different from Southern Arizona and the heat."

"Yeah, it does seem so much more scenic up here than down around Tucson. That still would not stop me from visiting our new friends the Purdues again. I liked the way they treated us, Tom, and it felt good to have a mother and father again," Jacob told his friend.

"Me too! I could feel their kindness and sincerity." Tom laughed while he carefully watched the winding highway road.

As they continued to drive, Jacob was deep in thought, thinking of how good it will be for Buck and Angie and Tom all living at the LL Ranch with his family. Ole Cooter will welcome the help with ranch and animals. Maybe they could take regular vacations and visit the Purdues now that they have established friends in Arizona.

The drive to the chief's home on the reservation took about a half hour with the hilly mountain roads. When they arrived, they saw a group of twenty or so kids playing football together, and they briefly stopped to stare at the three trucks driving along.

They drove up a dirt road to a large house that had a large wooden front porch and a big older-looking long-haired man walked out on the porch and waved them to greet him. Chaco waited for everyone to gather together so he could introduce them to his father. Tom and Jacob came walking up from behind everyone who had gathered on the front porch. "Everyone, this is my father, Chief Big Eagle!"

The chief looked at everyone and smiled, reaching out his hand to greet everyone. "I'm glad you all accepted my invitation to stay here for the night! Our home is your home, and I assure you, no reporters will bother you here."

Chaco's three sisters giggled from behind the chief, staring at Jacob and Tom Rivers. Tom held out his hand to the chief. "Sir, I'm of Choctaw descent from the reservation in Oklahoma. I'm honored to meet you and your family!"

The chief smiled at him. "Likewise, son. You are welcome in my home. And please forgive my daughters here. They know all about you and Jacob."

Chief Big Eagle and his wife went to great lengths to make their guests feel at home; they offered their hospitality for the evening until the final day of the rodeo was to begin in Sedona. Everyone felt relaxed and comfortable, and they laughed and enjoyed hearing the chief talk of the old days as a boy growing up in the reservation. "I joined the marines when I was sixteen years old, along with many of my friends. There were no jobs then, so we joined up."

Jacob spoke, "Did you go to war?"

"Well, first we went to boot camp in Camp Pendleton, California. After that, we were sent to the Mojave Desert for artillery training."

"You were very young," Tom said.

"Yes, many of us lied about our age to get in. We were sent to Iwo Jima and Okinawa to fight the Japanese." He drank some of his coffee. "The Japanese were very clever people. They started intercepting our radio transmissions and were bombing our locations, and so we started using Navajo names for different codes. We were known then as the Navajo code talkers, and they couldn't figure what we were doing."

"Sir, this is an honor to speak with you. We learned of these things in school. To be in the presence of a code talker is an honor," Jacob spoke up.

"I became friends with Will Gibson on the island of Iwo Jima. We only had 250 men to fight a huge Japanese force, and we were two of only twenty-seven men who survived that encounter. I was one of the four men who raised the American flag when it was over."

"My goodness!" Sarah said, holding her hand over her mouth.

"We fought for our country, and many of us died over there. And when we came home, we weren't even allowed to vote until 1949."

Everyone sat quietly and somewhat stunned at what they just heard. The chief was a courageous, humble, and kind man who had extended his home for strangers because of his friendship with Will Gibson.

Later that evening, they all went down to the stream and fished for trout. Tom gave them instructions on how he caught fish in Oklahoma with his parents using just a bamboo pole and a fishing line. It was just what everyone needed to relieve the stress of the next day's events at the rodeo.

Lying together on a soft and grassy hill just watching the kid's fish, Sarah turned to her Luke. "Honey, I want you to keep an eye on Jacob tomorrow, okay? The things Will told us about Millie and her bad cowboys scare me to death."

Luke patted her on the hand, "Of course I will, sweetheart!"

Her voice was quivering. "I don't know what I would do if anything happened to our baby."

"Baby?" Luke chuckled. "What baby are you talking about?"

Sarah gave him a stern look. "Luke, to Jenny and I, Jacob will always be that baby we took care of all his life. We both helped Rory and Millie care for and raised that little guy. Rory was so very proud of his son!" She gazed into the sky.

Luke wrapped his arms around her. "Sweetheart, I promise to guard Jacob with my life. Don't forget, hon, I love him too. I've known him since he was four years old, remember?"

Sarah hugged him. "I know, honey. I'm sorry, and I do know that!" She kissed him on the cheek.

Meanwhile, Jacob stood alongside the creek where some were fishing, and he was throwing a football with Chaco and a few of his friends. The Navajo boys were in awe of the Wonder Kid from Tyler. He was having fun and feeling very relaxed, just like he was on vacation up in the mountains of Northern Arizona. And by 9:30 that night, everyone was in bed, sleeping and getting rest for the next day's events. The chief had warned them to stay covered up because the crisp mountain air was sometimes very brisk.

Before falling fast asleep, Jacob had prayed to the Lord to work everything out for everyone. He prayed for the chief and his family and the people on the Navajo reservation. He prayed for Jim and Georgia Purdue, that their children would come home and be closer to their parents. And he prayed for the cowboys and all the animals in the rodeo, that no harm would come to them. As he fell asleep, he dreamt about the times that he and his dad would go riding together for hours at a time out in the fields far from any people—just him and his dad.

The next morning, everyone rose from their comfortable beds, and they could smell the flapjacks and oatmeal cooking in the kitchen. Georgia and the girls were in the kitchen, helping the chief's wife and daughters with breakfast. Chaco was so happy to have such friendly guest staying at their home, and his father allowed some of his good friends to stay and enjoy these moments with him.

While they ate, Jacobs's manager Jim Rogers and the chief discussed the plans for the day. "I'll have Buck and Tom on the alert for any trouble. By Saturday, we can start thinking about heading home," Jim told the chief.

Jenny teased her brother. "Oh, Jacob, you look so handsome! Were all so proud of you, young man!"

Smiling, the chief spoke up, "Luke, my young warriors will be all around the arena today, and they will assist you, watching for any trouble. If Millie's thugs get through, they won't do it easily."

Luke smiled at him. "Thank you, sir! I think we can pull this off today and tomorrow on the last day, and then, we can load up Tuff and go back home."

Jim Purdue spoke up as he sat next to Georgia, who had sat down to eat, "Jacob, I know you have to be feeling some pressure right now, but hold on. That's what I would tell my kids. You'll make it just fine."

Jacob sat his spoon down after swallowing some oatmeal and drank some hot tea. "Thank you, Jim and Georgia, for everything. You're swell!"

After an excellent breakfast, everyone had finished getting cleaned up, and Chief Big Eagle had them loaded up in the trucks for the drive to the rodeo grounds. Jacobs's first event, the steer wrestling, would start at 8:30.

Just as Jim had planned, the news and camera crews were anxiously waiting at the front gates to the rodeo grounds as Jacob's people arrived. Several had pushed their way through the crowds with their assistants carrying their camera equipment and were stopped by the chief and Jim Rogers. "Sir, sir, can we get an interview with the famous Wonder Kid, please?" they asked.

Buck and Tom stood in front of Jacob to protect him. "Buck, it's okay. They can have just one interview each, and then we have to get going," Jim intervened.

The man smiled and pushed a microphone toward Jacob. "Just a quick word, Mr. Bramble. Are you nervous about the final event of this year?"

Jacob hesitated a moment before he shyly answered, "No, sir, not at all. I've waited two years to go home, and I'm ready."

The next man spoke up, pushing his microphone toward Jacob, "What about Ty Herder, Jacob? Is he a significant threat to you today? And then there's the great Brent Stead from Kingsport, Tennessee. He's hot right now!"

Jacob smiled. "Ty Herder is going to get spanked today! The great Brent Stead is a good ole boy from Tennessee, and I think highly of him. I would rather lose to Brent!" He laughed and walked away, being led by his family and friends.

From a distance, Ty Herder and Millie watched the people and reporters swarm the Brambles. "There he is, Millie. I'll be danged if I'm going to lose to that rookie. You need to get more help to stop him, do you hear me?"

"We will. Don't worry, cutie! I'll take care of it."

There were cowboys from all over the country, and some had been watching Jacob being interviewed and liked him; some did not. When the Brambles finally worked their way through the crowds, they made it to Will Gibson's trailer and started getting Jacob and his gear prepared for the first event of steer wrestling. Chaco and Tom brought the big black roan horse and his tack all decked out and ready for Jacob.

Jim Rogers and the chief walked around the arena, getting the feel of the crowds, and then went up to the top of the bleachers to the enclosed glass VIP booth. They had placed the chief's young warriors in strategic places to guard against any attacks from Millie and her hired cowboys.

Jacob was warming up, throwing the football around with Chaco and Tom while Buck brushed down the black and kept him calm. The fans were being held back by security as they watched the three boys tossing the ball back and forth.

Jim had come down to talk with Buck, who was still holding the black roan for Jacob.

CHAPTER 9

"Any signs of Millie yet, Buck?"

"No, I haven't seen hide or hair of them, Jim, but I'll keep an eye out for trouble. Don't worry," Buck said with a sullen look on his face.

Patting Buck on the shoulder, Jim said, "Okay, Buck, let's pull this off as smoothly as we can. I've never been more nervous in the last two years with this boy of ours, and I'll be glad when it's all over. Jacob had done so well for all of us. We owe him a lot. I'll tell you the truth, Buck, I feel guilty and couldn't sleep well last night."

"Me too, Jim, but why did you have trouble sleeping?"

Jim wiped his forehead with his handkerchief and his eyes. "Well, I've grown fond of Jacob. I kind of feel like I have taken advantage of his talent in a way. At the time I met him, I was selling stock because I didn't have anyone wanting me to manage them. I saw this kid as a second chance for me."

"It's a little different for me. I knew his dad well, and he was naive but honest. It was clear to everyone there that he didn't deserve to be in prison. Reilly Rider knew Campbell and Ellie Bramble and knew their son Rory was of good stock."

Jim's lip shook with tears. "You know, Buck, I don't even care about the championship. What have we done to this kid? All he ever wanted was to rekindle the memories of his dad through that big Brahma. That poor boy!" He started crying.

Buck hugged Jim. "You love him, don't you, Jim? Like a son."

"Yes, I guess I do, Buck"—turning his head to hide his tears.

Buck smiled. "Well, what should we do?"

They both looked over at Jacob, who was laughing and talking with Tom and Chaco like he was with his two brothers, throwing the ball around and having a good time. They watched for a few minutes and looked at the fans behind the roped-off area, who seemed to love him, then Jim said, "He wants to finish the race and go home, Buck. Let's help him finally get back to his home!"

Jacob finished his warm-up routine, and he took the time to put his new chaps before climbing up on the black roan. Buck hollered up to him, "Okay, kiddo! Let's get this done and go home to the LL Ranch, okay?"

Jacob smiled. "That's the words I wanted to hear, Buck!"

As Tom Rivers led the black to the stall for the takeoff, they paused and listened to the announcer on the loudspeaker, telling the results of the events as they took place.

When Tom had Jacob in the stall, waiting for the gate to swing open, the announcer spoke, "Okay, folks, for you in the stands here today and the countless fans who are watching from television around the world, here he is, the grandson of the late rodeo legend Campbell Bramble. Give a warm welcome for the Wonder Kid from Tyler, Texas. The twenty-year-old Texan who has swept the nation as a rookie going all the way to the top! Give a warm welcome for Jacob John Bramble!" And the crowds went wild.

As the gate swung open, the black roan ran out into the arena, carrying Jacob, who was swinging his lasso rope around and around in the air as he closed in on the steer. He aimed it and threw the rope, and it landed around the steer's head as the roan skidded to a stop, pulling backward. Jacob quickly jumped off the black and ran over and grabbed the steer's two horns and pulled it down to the ground. He stood up, throwing his hands in the air, signaling he was done, and the buzzer sounded off, and it was over.

The crowd screamed in delight, hearing the announcer telling them it was the fastest time so far. He had given them what they wanted and ran over to the gate and jumped up and over it, landing quickly on the other side and was greeted by Buck. Tom had retrieved the black, pulling him back behind the gates. "Great job, son!" Buck told him.

Luke stood close by on alert for any trouble. As a sheriff, he knew Millie's cowboys meant business, and he wasn't having any of it. A Mexican cowboy approached Luke and appeared to be friendly. "Hello, sir."

"Hello," Luke replied.

"I just wanted to let you know, some of us competitors like Jacob Bramble. We are not in with Ty Herder and that woman he hangs with."

Luke smiled, putting his hands on his hips. "Why are you telling me this, young man?"

"Several reasons, mister. Ty was asking for men to make it difficult for Jacob from winning today. Second, some of us have had dealings with Ty before in other arenas, and we don't like him."

"That's good information. Thank you, son!"

The cowboy took his hat off and wiped the sweat from his head and placed the hat back on. "Brent Stead and I saw two clowns over by the concession stands, mister. One of them is that woman Ty hangs with. Brent wanted me to warn you."

Luke looked around the grounds and took a deep breath. "Well, I do appreciate that news. I'll take care of it!" He shook hands with the cowboy, and the young man walked away. Luke went over to Buck and informed him as Jacob made another good run with the steer wrestling. The stadium scoreboard flashed lively colored lights: "The Wonder Kid does it again."

Ty Herder was running in second place against Jacob, and Brent Stead was bringing up a close third place. The fans were ecstatic over Jacobs's performance; he was giving them what they had come here for. As the day went on, cowboy after cowboy was thrown, kicked, and dragged by the bucking horses and Brahmas. The sun was hot, and the dust was flying all over the rodeo grounds. Chief Big Eagle had gathered all his young warriors together to watch out for Jacob.

In the chute again, Tom Rivers held the black for Jacob as he climbed on its back. Slowly, he leaned over and whispered into her ears, "Hold on, sweetheart. You've served me well today, and I'm almost done." He patted her head and hugged her.

"Jacob, hold your head up when you jump on that steer. His horns are awfully long," Tom warned his friend.

"Thank you, Tom!" He smiled back.

The gate swung open, and the steer ran fast in front of the black. Jacob wasted no time in running to catch up and roped its horns again. He jumped off of the horse and grabbed the big long horns of the steer. He twisted and turned, and down went the steer, and he held it down for a few seconds, and the buzzer sounded off, and the crowd went wild. Jacob stood up and patted the steer on the rump, then he looked around the big arena; everywhere he turned, there were cameras pointing at him, but he didn't care. He waved at the fans and ran to the rails and threw himself up and over.

He took the time to stop and watch Brent Stead wrestle the next steer and waited for the buzzer to sound. Brent ran to the rails and threw himself over, standing next to Jacob. "The suns hot today, huh Jacob?" He smiled.

Jacob smiled back and reached out to shake his hand. "Yes, sir. Glad to be in the same rodeo with you Kingsport boys. You're the best, Brent. I'm proud to sharing the arena with you."

Brent grinned. "I should be saying that to you, Jacob. My grandfather told me all about Campbell Bramble. I'm proud to know you!" They shook hands and parted ways.

Hours later, with the day winding down, Jacob was finished with the saddle bronco riding, the steer roping, and the bareback competition. This would be his third ride on the Brahma Whirlwind, the tough bull from Colorado. The animal was so angry in the chute after Tom and Buck had tightened his flank strap, Jacob was having some trouble getting his left hand gripped around the bull rope. It jumped up and down and turned abruptly, pinning Jacob against the stall until Tom managed to get him calmed down.

Jacob, determined to continue, leaned over the rails and grabbed the bull's ears and whispered his secret talk to him, and the animal seemed to calm down some. And then the gate swung open, and out flew the Brahma, jumping and twisting and kicking his hind legs in the sir in an attempt to kick off the flank strap. He leaped high in the air in circles, trying to throw Jacob, then he stumbled and fell on the ground, and the crowds screamed out in horror. Still holding on to the bull, the animal wiggled and got to his feet again and started again. Finally, the buzzer went off, and Jacob jumped off of the bull and ran to the side of the rails and threw himself up and over to the other side.

"Good Lord, Jacob. I thought he had you for a second. That Whirlwind is one tough bull!" Tom yelled out.

Jacob grinned and shrugged it off. "No big deal!"—walking to the exit gate. "Fellas, I have to go to the bathroom. I'll be right back!"

Tom smiled a nervous smile and waved to him but looked at Buck. "All that's left is one more Brahma ride, and he's done, Buck."

Buck smiled at Tom. "Don't worry! He's doing just fine. Give the boy some privacy, okay," he laughed.

"All right!" Tom answered back and continued what he was doing as Jacob came out of the temporary bathroom. Looking toward the barn, he saw his mother and brother go inside where Tuff was. Curious, he climbed over the rails of the arena and headed for the barn.

"Where are you going, Jacob?" Chaco yelled out to him.

He answered, "I'm going to see what those two are up to in there. If I don't come back, tell Luke and Buck where I went, okay, Chaco?"

Chaco looked worried, "Okay, I guess, but be careful, Jacob."

"I will just remember what I told you," Jacob called over his shoulder as he headed toward the barn, ignoring the stares from people watching him. Tom and Buck were unaware where he had gone.

Walking casually and trying not to attract attention, Jacob had made his way to the barn. He stopped by the front door and listened intently for sounds from inside, and then he went around to the side entrance and decided to try sneaking in. He opened the squeaky door, and the first thing he saw was his mother and Willie standing by Tuff's stall, and Willie had a cattle prod in his hand.

Quietly, he snuck through the hay bins and attempted to hide behind a stack of hay, and he was listening to his mother talk. Unable to make out what she was saying, he decided to move in closer when he heard Tuff moan with pain. Peeking from behind the haystack, he witnessed Willie poking the electric prodder in Tuff's face. Tuff would jerk backward with a cry of pain while Willie laughed.

Unable to stand still, he stepped out. "Stop it, Willie!" Jacob yelled out with a determined look upon his face.

"You know what, Jacob? You might be somebody to those idiots in the bleachers out there, but to me, you're nothing but a dumb hick from Tyler." Willie looked at him with hate in his eyes.

"You're just like your father—soft-hearted," Millie spit out scornfully.

"I'll always be proud of my father for teaching me good things about life." Jacobs's eyes were blazing.

"Look, mother, he's getting angry," Willie laughed.

Just then, Jacob heard rustling all around him. He looked around and saw that he was being surrounded by cowboys who had been hiding in the shadows of the barn. There were at least seven mean-looking cowboys around him; he realized he had been set up by his mother and brother.

"See, I told you he would come in here if he saw us hanging around the dumb animal," she bragged with a smile.

"Okay, Millie, now we can finish our business with Jacob here." Ty Herder looked at Jacob standing alone against seven men.

"Well, well, the Wonder Kid who can't be thrown from any animal on God's green earth. Is that right?" Ty swaggered up to Jacob, eyeing him up and down. "You don't look so tough to me, boy," Ty said. "Remember the first time I saw you in Amarillo? Well, I do."

"I could whip you with one hand tied behind my back with my eyes closed," Jacob deliberately insulted him.

Ty looked at him with hatred in his eyes. "Oh, can you?"—sneering. "With one hand and no eyes, huh?" He laughed and spat on the floor.

Millie interrupted them. "I think it's time for us to go now, Willie."

"No, you go ahead, mother. I'll catch up to you," Willie told her while he held the electric prodder close to Jacobs's face.

"What are you going to do, Willie?" she asked with a worried look on her face.

"Don't worry! I'm not going to permanently maim him," he answered.

Jacob watched his mother turn and walk away. "You walked out on my father too. I don't want ever to hear your name mentioned again!" he screamed.

Millie looked back at Jacob and laughed, and then she opened the door and squeezed out, leaving one of the thugs to close and lock it behind her. Chaco watched Millie come out of the barn alone and ran to tell Buck and Tom what was happening.

Luke just happened to be talking with Buck when Chaco ran to them. "Buck, Tom, Luke, you must come quickly. Jacob went into Tuff's barn. He did not come out."

Meanwhile, back inside of the barn, Ty Herder was trying to decide what to do with Jacob. "So, you can beat me with one hand?" Ty asked again.

"Well, I know that if you thought you could handle me alone, you would not have brought all these girls to help you," Jacob taunted.

Willie poked Jacob in the side with the prodder, causing him to flinch with pain, but he did not make a sound. "Willie, I'm going to give you the butt kicking I should have years ago."

Willie looked at him. "You are? Well, let's see." He tried to poke Jacob again and recoiled in surprise when Jacob grabbed the prodder and quickly took it away from him. Now Jacob had a weapon in his hand.

Jacob threw it on the floor then looked at Ty. "Are you going to interfere while I'm kicking his butt?" He pointed to Willie.

"No," Ty answered, "I never liked the whining sissy anyway."

Just then, Willie ran at Jacob and threw a wild right. Jacob calmly moved aside, sticking his foot out at the last minute and tripped Willie, causing him to fall clumsily to the ground. Standing back, Jacob gave his brother the time to stand up, and Willie charged him again, but this time Jacob hit him with a solid punch to the stomach, knocking the wind out of him.

Before Willie could catch his breath, Jacob had grabbed him by the hair and gave a hard forearm across his chest, knocking him to the ground again, and he lay there stunned. Jacob stood straight up, waiting to be jumped by one of Ty's men. He figured these cowboys had been hired to hurt him, and they wanted to get paid.

Ty backed up and said, "I have to go ride in this last event now. You guys finish him off and make sure he only has one hand, and his eyes are closed. Then I'll be back." He backed slowly toward the barn door; he unlocked it and crept outside.

Before the door shut, Willie had run out. From a distance, Luke, Tom, and Buck watched Ty and Willie leave quickly, and panic struck them as they realized that after all of their precautions, they had let Jacob slip away from them.

When they arrived at the barn, they found the door shut and locked, and they could not open it. "They don't want Jacob to leave. Then he will miss the last event of the day, and he will lose," Buck told them.

Luke yelled out, "I think that's what Ty and Millie had counted on all along. They waited for their moment and took advantage when Jacob was alone."

"No, they lured him into the barn. I saw them, and Jacob went in through the side entrance," Chaco told them.

Tom Rivers ran around to the side and came back. "It's locked, but I could hear muffled sounds like a struggle is going on." He had a feeling his friend was in trouble.

Sarah and Jenny and the Purdues had arrived. "What's going on, boys?" Jim Purdue asked. "What's wrong with the door locked?"

Chaco quickly explained what had happened when Jim Rogers and Chief Big Eagle arrived with Will Gibson. "There's a window up there," Will pointed high over the door.

Chaco and his three friends formed a ladder, and he climbed up and stood on their shoulders, and he could see inside. "I see him. Jacob is surrounded by some cowboys."

"How many are there, Chaco?" Tom asked frantically.

"I count six that I can see, and poor Jacob is alone except for Tuff."

Sarah screamed out, "Is he all right? What are they doing?"

Chaco hesitated for a second then said, "Yes, he looks fine, except it seems like they are getting ready to jump him. He's surrounded on all sides."

"You need to get that door opened, Will!" Jenny yelled out.

Buck and Tom looked at each other helplessly; they were locked out and unable to help him. "Will," Luke screamed out, "go to the trailer and get your truck. We might be able to ram the door to open it."

Will Gibson ran off toward the trailer and after a few minutes had driven back with the truck.

"Chaco, tell us when Jacob has cleared away from the doors. If we ram it, he may get hurt," Luke yelled up to him.

Chaco yelled back, "Hold on, he's too close to the door right now."

As they waited, they heard the announcer calling out Brent Stead's score. Then they heard Ty's name called over the loudspeaker; he was riding the bull Moody Blues. Millie had been smarter than they had given her credit for; so far, she had been successful at trapping Jacob, and at this point, it looked as though he could miss the final event.

As Luke and Will were devising a plan to get the door open, Chaco yelled down to them, "Their fighting, now Tom. Two of those guys just jumped Jacob from behind."

"It's started," Buck relayed with an emotional tone. "It seems like no matter what protective measures we took, they still managed to get to Jacob."

Tom added, "I don't like this one bit." He pounded on the door with his fist.

"Hey! Jacob is holding his own so far, and they don't seem to be able to get a hold of him. He is moving and punching anyone that comes close to him," Chaco yelled down to them.

"Get 'em, Jacob!" Sarah and Jenny gave each other a high five.

Inside the barn, Jacob was being rushed one man at a time. They planned to wear him down so they could work him over when he tired. They knew he was the best rodeoer in the country, and rumor was that he had been an all-state varsity football player in high school.

To the dismay of the cowboys, Jacob did not tire so quickly. He was in great cardiovascular as well as physical conditioning. He could go on fighting for a long time, and his assailants soon found this out. Trying to catch him from behind, one of the cowboys ran at Jacob with a wild right swing. He leaned left, and with his boots, spurs, and all kicked the man in the groin. Then Jacob turned, and from the side, he kicked another one in the face, sending him crashing to the floor with a cry of pain.

A third man came at him, allowing no time to rest or catch his breath. He swung on Jacob wildly, but Jacob stood back and waited for the swing, then he swung hard and punched the guy in the face three or four times until the cowboy fell backward, unconscious.

He was rushed again by two more men, one of whom managed to grab hold of his arm, pulling him off balance. At the same time, the other man dove down and grabbed Jacob's legs. Jacob kicked the one attacking his legs in the face, making him let go, allowing Jacob to easily pull the other face first into a wooden post.

Again, one of them rushed him, and he punched the guy in the face, felling him on the spot. Not giving them time to launch another attack on him, Jacob ran straight at the remaining eight men who were still standing. "Come on!" he screamed out in anger. "I'll take all of you on"—screaming crazily.

Realizing they could not beat him without some help, several of them got some small two-by-four pieces of lumber and came at him swinging. Jacob lunged at one who had fire in his eyes and blocked the swinging board with his left wrist; the bone shattered with the impact.

Ignoring the pain, Jacob swung a hard right and decked the man, sending him to the floor just as another one hit in the back with his two-by-four. As Jacob staggered forward, two of the cowboys grabbed him by the arms and slammed his face into the double doors of the barn. Dazed and feeling a strange numbness in his wrist, he was wheeled around and punched again and again in the face and the ribs. They held him against the door, laughing as they took turns hitting him.

One of the cowboys raised a hand for the others to stop the beating. "Hold it, fellas. Ty said to make sure he couldn't see and that he only has one hand to fight with. Look at his face. Both of his eyes are swollen shut, and his nose is broken in several places. Quick, get him up and bring him over to that rail by the stall."

Three of them dragged his limp body over to the rail, placing his left arm over the fence and two of them took turns kicking the arm. After several kicks, Jacob lifted his head slowly, tears of pain flowed down his face, but he did not cry out. His lip quivered as he pleaded to himself, "Help me, Dad. Please help me!" Then his head dropped forward in exhaustion as he fought to stay conscious.

"What did he say?" one of them asked.

With a laugh, one of them said, "I think he is crying for his daddy! The "Wonder Kid" is crying for his daddy." They all laughed, but then they stopped abruptly. They turned when they heard a loud roaring and snorting coming from the Brahma's stall, and suddenly, fear came upon all of them when they realized the bull had reacted to Jacob's crying. The bull became very agitated, moving back and forth in an aggressive manner. Suddenly, he backed up and charged the gate and broke through. Tuff screamed as he ran straight at the cowboys, turning his head from side to side as if he was trying to gore them with his long full horns.

Outside, Chaco was screaming out loud, "Tuff has escaped his stall and is chasing the cowboys away from Jacob. They're running from him!"

"Oh, my goodness! What's going on in there?" Sarah yelled to Luke

"It looks like Tuff is defending Jacob! Can you believe this? That Bull is chasing the bad guys," Chaco announced to them.

Tuff was running wildly through the barn, herding the cowboys away from Jacob. He charged two of the men who didn't have time to move earlier; one of them picked up a pitchfork and jabbed it at Tuff, daring him to charge. Tuff accepted the challenge and charged him with his head down and his horns aimed right at his target. The man dashed and dropped the pitchfork and ran away.

Jacob had fallen to the floor, barely conscious, and he was a bloody mess with both swollen eyes shut and his face badly bruised. His nose was broken, and his shirt had been stripped off after they had whipped him with a leather strap.

Chaco was still reporting from the high window above, "Look at that Brahma go. He's chasing those cowboys all over the barn, and he's run over several of them."

Then he became silent; a large lump had formed in his throat at the sight of Jacob lying on the floor, and from a distance, he looked dead. "Jacob's lying on the floor, and he's not moving at all."

Will Gibson reacted to hearing that. "Okay, Luke, I'm not waiting anymore. I'm going in." He threw his truck into gear and started to move forward when suddenly, the front door to the barn flew open, and out came the cowboys running in all directions.

They didn't get far when Tom and Buck and Luke, with the help of the warriors, grabbed them and quickly tied them up with rope. One of them lunged at Tom, and he stepped aside and kicked the guy in the stomach and elbowed him in the back, causing him to fall on his face.

Just then, they heard the announcer on the loudspeaker call Ty Herder's time on the bull ride, placing him in second place ahead of Brent Stead. "Ladies and gentleman, we have what all of you have been waiting for all day. The last contestant in this rodeo is none other than the 'Wonder Kid' and possibly the best rodeoer in the entire world today."

The crowds roared in delight, and when Jacob did not appear, they became silent. Jim Rogers and Chief Big Eagle stood up in concern; both of them walked up to the big glass window and looked out, trying to see what was happening down below.

Millie and Willie hid behind the concession stand, listening and waiting to hear the good news. "Our boys must have done their jobs, Willie. If Jacob doesn't show even though he's in the lead, he will forfeit the championship for not competing in the final event."

Willie snickered along with her. "Cool! Now, Ty will win and give us half of the prize money, right?"

"You're darn right he will. He knows not to mess with me." She had no problem causing more trouble if she had to just to get what she wanted.

There were scuffles all over the barnyard as the chief's warriors made sure the cowboys were secure enough to hold them until the local sheriffs arrived.

Back in the barn, Tuff had wandered back over to Jacob who still lay unconscious. He hovered anxiously over the still body of the young man he had so bravely defended, panting loudly with moisture dripping from his nose. In a matter of seconds, Jacob's concerned family and friends ran into the barn to assist him. Jenny reached down and felt his neck for a pulse. "He has a pulse. He's alive!" She breathed a quick prayer and picked up Jacob's hand in her own.

Sarah leaned down with Jenny. "Jacob, can you hear me?"—nudging his arm.

"Yes, Sarah, I can hear you." He could not open his swollen eyes, but he did manage a smile through all the pain for his sisters.

"Jacob, they just called your name over the loudspeaker. If you don't show up, they will disqualify you," Sarah told him.

Tom leaned over and handed Jenny a tin cup of fresh water. Together, they managed to get him to take a couple of sips. "He's in no condition to go on. We're going to have to call it, Buck," Tom spoke up.

"I know, Tom, and he can't even see out of his eyes, and his left arm and wrist are broken. There is no way he can ride anymore today." Buck stood up and looked at the others. It would be up to him to tell the officials that Jacob could no longer compete.

Jacob heard Buck talking and managed to get his attention and feebly protested, "No, Buck, I didn't come this far and spend two years away from my family to walk away and let Ty and my mother win today."

Buck stopped and looked at Jacob as they heard the ambulance arriving. "But, Jacob, you're real hurt bad, son."

Jacob glanced upward toward heaven. "Jesus, forgive those men what they did to me. But don't let them win like this. I know a little boy who is in the hospital that is braver than me. If you could give me a little more strength, I want to finish this battle."

Georgia Purdue smiled and looked around at everyone in the room. "He's praying and asking Jesus for help."

Tuff stood calmly and patiently next to Jacob, looking as though he were listening to his words. Tom looked at the animal in awe; he had never seen anything like this before. This Brahma is acting as a loyal, well-trained dog.

Jacob reached out with his right arm. "Help me get on Tuff, and I can still make my time."

"Jacob, no!" Jenny cried out.

"Yes, somebody help me on my dad's back, and he will know what to do. Dad will help me through Tuff. I know he is watching me right now!"

"He's in shock!" Will Gibson spoke up. "Let's wait for the ambulance to get here."

"No!" Jacob screamed out in a loud, piercing voice. "I said someone help me now!" And he reached for Tuff, who seemed to stand still, waiting for him. "I only have a few seconds to get out there. Do you guys hear me?"

Not knowing what else to do, Tom and Buck lifted him on, and Jacob gripped the bull rope with his right hand, and Sarah wiped the blood from his face with a wet towel. He whispered something in her ear, and she smiled at him. Jenny put his cowboy hat on his head, astonished that Tuff stood still, wagging his tail.

Sarah turned and ran off as Buck spoke to Jacob, "Okay, buddy!"

He and Tom lifted Jacob and set him on Tuff's calming, secure back. "This is your ball game. Go ahead and do what you do best. This is the last event of the year, and you can finally go home," Buck encouraged him.

Tuff instinctively turned and slowly walked out of the barn with the ambulance paramedics and the sheriffs watching. The Brahma walked through the crowds to the arena, carrying the Wonder Kid on his back. The bull seemed to know exactly where he was going, and no one tried to stop him. One of the chief's warriors was waiting at the gate and opened it, allowing Tuff to enter. People mumbled but kept quiet, watching the miracle unravel right in front of their eyes.

The crowds were shocked to see Jacob's bloody back from the brutal whipping he had endured, and he was barely able to hold his left arm and wrist up, and his eyes were swollen shut. The arena became quiet, watching in horror as the announcer spoke on the loudspeaker, "Folks, I don't know who is responsible for this terrible act of violence on Jacob, but here he is—the Wonder Kid from Tyler, Texas.

"He is riding the fierce and mighty Brahma bull called The Raging Tornado from California. I was just informed that this last ride is dedicated to a sick boy, who is staying in the Mount Sinai Hospital in New York City, who, according to Jacob Bramble, is the bravest young man he ever met—Ethan Grant III!"

Tuff walked into the middle of the arena without a flank strap on and took a little jump off the ground and kicked a couple of times, and the bell sounded off, and it was over. The fans went wild! Jacob had done what the newspapers and talk show host had predicted, and he had won the professional rodeo world championship title.

Tuff stopped and calmly walked back out of the gate where Sarah and Jenny waited for him, crying profusely. Tom and Buck, with the help of Luke, helped Jacob get down off of Tuff. At that instant, Jacob felt compelled with a strange feeling form down inside of him. He yelled for Chaco to bring him his footballs as everyone stared at him. "Chaco, I'm going to throw three Hail Maries, okay? After I throw one, hand me the others as quick as you can, okay?"

"Sure thing, Jacob." Chaco was just as confused as the others hearing this. As the television cameras filmed everything that was happening, his entourage stood back and said nothing.

"God, guide my arm," Jacob quietly mumbled as he drew back and threw the football toward the opposite side of the arena where Millie and her constituents were lurking. Quickly, Chaco handed him another, and he threw it high in the air, and then another. As the audience in the stands were watching, the footballs soared like he had thrown a ball on the football field.

Across the arena, Millie turned in disgust; she pushed Willie out of her way. "Move you, idiots. Let's get out of here!" She was hit with a football with such a force, she dropped to the ground.

Ty and Willie saw what happened, and both of them started laughing. Just as Ty was going to give Willie a high five, he was also hit in the head with a football, and he fell to the ground unconscious.

It took Willie a couple of seconds to realize what had happened when a third football hit him on the head, knocking him to the ground unconscious too.

The fans in the stands had watched the local sheriffs apprehend all three of them. The media was having a field day with the live coverage; they had it on tape for all the world to see. They knew this exciting finale would cause the ratings to soar. The whole stadium was in an uproar, and the "Wonder Kid" had not only taken the world title from Ty Herder, he had done the impossible by hitting all three targets from at least one hundred yards while blind and with a broken arm and wrist.

Luke and Buck went over to the other side and assisted the sheriffs in arresting Millie and her two culprits. They were all three arrested for conspiracy to commit a crime, kidnapping, assault, battery, and attempted murder.

Will Gibson assisted the paramedics in helping Jacob, and they put him on a stretcher and loaded him into the ambulance and whisked him away to the Sedona Medical Center. He had to miss the final rodeo ceremonies due to his injuries.

The doctors were appalled at Jacobs's condition; they carefully checked him over and documented the many injuries he had sustained. In their examination, they found he had many apparent cuts and bruises, two fractured ribs, and a punctured lung. He had a broken nose and a fractured arm and wrist, and he suffered from internal bleeding. The doctors could not figure out how he finished the rodeo and how he possibly was able to throw those footballs.

After he had come out of emergency surgery, he slept for three days without waking once. On the fourth day, he awoke and told them he was hungry and wanted to go home. Maryann had flown out to Sedona and was waiting at his side; she had sat by his bed for three days.

Finally, he was released from the hospital, and Luke and the girls arrived to pick him up. They wheeled him out of the front door, and he could see again, but he was still black and blue. He was greeted by a barrage of well-wishers; he could see several hundred people had come from all over Arizona to wish him well. There were people holding up banners about him and people waving and cheering for him. The media had their cameras set, and photographers were taking pictures. Maryann stood by his side. "Jacob, you're a hero to these people! They were all very concerned about you."

Luke looked at him. "Millie and Ty and Willie are in jail. They are facing some severe charges, and I don't think they will get out of jail."

Brent Stead walked up to him. "I'm happy you're better, Jacob. Anytime you come to Kingsport, Tennessee, you come to have a meal with my family. My neighbors will be jealous a celebrity will be in my house." He laughed. "It was an honor to compete with the Kid from Tyler!"

Jacob reached up and shook his hand and smiled. "Thank you, Brent, and God bless!" He turned and looked for Tom and Buck. He saw them and the Purdues standing next to the truck and trailer, and they had Tuff in the trailer waiting to go.

The six o'clock anchor from the Flagstaff news station put her microphone in his face. "Are you ready to go home after all you have been through, Jacob?"

Jacob took a breath of fresh air into his lungs. "I'm ready to go home and sign up for school. It's time I finished my education."

He looked at Chaco and Chief Big Eagle and many of the people from the reservation smiling and waving at him, and he waved back. He looked back at the hospital staff that was standing behind him, then he looked up to heaven and smiled. "Thank you, Lord, for all my blessings! And thank you, Dad, for all you taught me."

He stood up from the wheelchair, and with Maryann's help, she held his hand as he walked down the steps of the medical center into the awaiting crowds. Slowly, he reached out with his right hand and shook people's hands as he walked toward the truck. He walked and smiled with a Texas pride tickled inside that the reporters hailed him as one of the greatest athletes in the world.

The end!

ABOUT THE AUTHOR

Randy Lee Purdy is a self-taught writer and has been writing for twenty-five years. Born and raised in Terre Haute, Indiana, with six siblings and being a middle child, he moved to Tucson, Arizona, at the age of fifteen, and at the age of seventeen, he proudly served in the United States Army for a six-year obligation. He has worked many jobs, including medic in the army, air force reserve, an underground copper miner, school custodian, dishwasher, and a local car wash.

One memory at the car wash was being twenty years old fresh out of the army, except for being in the reserves. He was drying off the cars as they came off of the assembly line. To his amazement, a popular Hollywood actor came walking up to him as he dried his car off. He spoke with him in a stern tone, and he asked him how he had spent many years playing different parts that people loved. He responded to him, saying he only did what God had directed him to do. He told him that when you honor God, he will have a special walk all through life with us. He encouraged him to work hard and follow his dreams and God will do the rest. He never forgot his words.

Randy spent thirty-six years working in governmental positions as well. He has been a father, husband, grandfather, son, and brother to many family members. He has thoroughly enjoyed honoring God with simple fictional faith-based stories. He mixes history with American folklore and tries to capture the reader's attention with an honest attempt to capture their hearts. You have to become the person you are writing about to really get the attention of the reader.

He has been a sinner and a Christian man. That's what makes him understand how to have his characters succeed. Life to him is about good, honest work and honoring our parents who have sacrificed so much for us.

He is an animal lover that believes animals were created by God to love us, and he has had many that he has loved with all his heart. When we treat them good, God is happy with us.

His stories always include valuable relationships with God's animals. His life has always been to love his mother and father, never faltering to honor them. Family means everything to him, and he has always had strong family bonds and has been very blessed to have brothers and a sister who have always loved and supported him.

CPSIA information can be obtained
at www.ICGtesting.com
Printed in the USA
FSHW010757270420
69515FS